night

night

Vedrana Rudan

Translation by Celia Hawkesworth

Dalkey Archive Press
Normal · London

First published in Croatian as *Uho, grlo, nož* by AGM, 2002
Copyright © 2002 by Vedrana Rudan
Translation copyright © 2004 by Celia Hawkesworth

First edition, 2004
All rights reserved

Library of Congress Cataloging-in-Publication Data available
ISBN: 1-56478-347-2

Partially funded by a grant from the Illinois Arts Council,
a state agency.

Dalkey Archive Press is a nonprofit organization located in
Milner Library at Illinois State University and distributed in the
UK by Turnaround Publisher Services Ltd. (London).

www.centerforbookculture.org

Printed on permanent/durable acid-free paper and bound in
the United States of America.

Prologue

'Tonka, you have to explain to someone outside of it all who *you* are and who *they* are.'

'Why?'

'So an outsider can understand.'

'But it's all quite simple. I'm Tonka, last name Babić, I'm lying in bed, fooling with the TV remote. It's the middle of the night and I'm tired. I keep changing the channel.'

'And who are *they*?'

'They're all around me.'

'Where?'

'In the room with me. In the air of the room, in my eyes, under my eyelids, in my nose, in my ear, in the cardboard box on the shelf in the closet where I keep my swimming suits and summer tops and Kiki's Bermuda shorts, in the Ikea bedside lamp, in the universe. They can't see me, I can't see them. They hear me, I hear them.'

'It would be far better if you were an actress on the stage, there's a television screen behind you, you're acting in a one-person play, and *they* are the audience who are listening to you. That would be much better.'

'No, it wouldn't. Who'd give a part to a woman over fifty? The night is long. Who could memorize such a long script? And who could put up with such a long performance? If *they* were a theater audience, they'd go home.'

'So why couldn't you be a guest on some night-time television show? Some kind of program where people talk about their terrible experiences. The kind of program everyone wants to watch. You're in the studio, lying in bed, you're nuts, you're talking crazy, and *they* are the people who sit at home and watch you all night. There's a television screen behind you, you press your remote and get the same story.'

'But I'm not nuts and I don't like those kinds of programs. What I like best on television are documentaries. About animals. I like hippopotamuses that lie in the water, looking at me with their little, cunning eyes. That's what I like. Get it? Why can't you understand? Who are you?'

'I'm Someone Outside It All.'

Let's get going

I'm looking at the Ikea clock on top of the TV. The television is on, but the sound is off. There are some old women talking about something or other. Or maybe they aren't old. They just have grey hair. And no teeth. I'd look like an old woman too, but every three weeks I pay Alexandra a hundred marks to dye my hair red. I've spent four thousand marks on dental work so I can laugh with my mouth open. But . . . I don't laugh like that. When I was fourteen, the dentist pulled out my top left incisor. For years I laughed with my mouth closed. We were poor. My mother, my grandmother, and I. I bought myself my left tooth for my twenty-fourth birthday. I didn't have a big smile even then. I still grin that way. I'm lying on the bed in Kiki's pyjamas. Striped. Benetton. And, you ask, what does the upper tooth have to do with pyjamas? What is the connection between pyjamas and a tooth? This constant explaining is exhausting! Trying to connect things. Finding the subject, predicate and object. Why should anything in my life have any connection with anything else? Why are you so obsessed with connections? Logic. Causes. Consequences. I'm telling you: I'm lying in bed, I'm wearing Kiki's pyjamas, I'm looking at the clock. What time is it? What's that got to do with anything? And under the clock is the television with a picture but no sound. None of this has any connection with anything. I'm giving you the facts. Your questions piss me off. And your impatience. And that you need to look for drama in my lying here. Something happened. Or is going to happen. Something must happen. Because neither of us has nerves of granite or any other stone. You're human beings who can put up with a lot, yes, but even your patience has a limit. So if I just go on lying and talking nonsense, if nothing happens, you'll tell me to go fuck myself. You're full of shit. What do you expect of me? I'm not Shakespeare or a popular writer. I'm Tonka. I'm simply lying in bed. And staring at the clock. Kiki's in Ljubljana. OK. Maybe there's some drama going on. I've decided, when this night fades . . . What a good word 'fades'! Good one. Good one! When this night ends, I'll leave my Kiki. Leave him. Lock the door behind me. Open a new chapter. Burn all my bridges. Screw the past. Kiki can go to hell. Walk out into a new morning. You're relieved. I can hear you. You're saying, Great, here's some drama after all. It's not just about a stupid bitch lying in bed in the middle of night—it's not the middle of the night at all—alone and awake for no reason. Something's bothering her. Come on! Let's hear it! What's up with you, you old cow? How do we know you're old? You have a sickly, trembling voice . . . We hear the shaking. Come on! Faster! Kiki drinks? Cheats on you? Doesn't fuck you anymore? Hits you? Why are you going? Are you crazy? Now? You're old! Think about it! You've got a husband, for God's sake! Hang on to him! Wait! Hold on! You're leaving? At your age? You're *not* fucking leaving! So why did the man of your life go away? What's he doing in Ljubljana while you lie around in his pyjamas? Why don't you like me? Why are you such cynical jerks? You're not interested in my story. Why are unhappy stories the only good ones? What do you want from me? Why are you hurrying me? I can't shove my whole life into three sentences just because you're in a hurry. What's the hurry? What's round the corner? Whose insane life are you going to look at next when you get yourselves out of my bed? Here. It's time for a little chocolate. Of course it drives me crazy that I can't live without my chocolate. Fucking candy bars. OK. I'm not going to go on about chocolate. It's distracting you. But it's important! Important? What's important? I'm leaving my husband and going off with my lover who is—a fact that will be important to you—twelve years younger than me. Tomorrow morning, at seven, when you'll be in your offices, stores, or beds because you're unemployed, or at the Job Center, or dying, or fucking some slut, or under your wife, or on top of your fat husband, or next to your skinny little lover, or in front of your fat-headed boss, an Italian, or German, or Austrian, or Hungarian, or . . . I'll be opening the door of my home to my young lover . . . What a word *home*! I'll have my little Samsonite bag in my hand, I won't give a fuck about all the little things that show you have a life, wedding photographs and my daughter Aki's first tooth. I'll throw myself into his arms and grab him by the balls with my left hand. Our neighbor Tomi will see me. He always sees everything, the old shit. He'll think I'm a slut standing there in the doorway of my own home. But he won't know, the old shit, that I'll only be a slut for a short time, a very short time. And then I'll become the owner of a new man. Officially. We'll get married. Yes. I'll have to get a divorce. So will he. Miki. Why a divorce? Why all the talking? And why is my lover called Miki, when my husband is Kiki? You think I'm playing with you? That I'm confusing you on purpose? That while I'm talking, I'm giving you a chance to mix up 'Miki' and 'Kiki'?

Actually, I'm letting you know there's not much difference between Kiki and Miki. I'm trying to tell you that all men are the same . . . You're real pricks! Why are you so obsessed with messages? I'm trying to tell you something? I want to confuse you? Do you ever think at all? Has it ever occurred to you that no one wants to send you any kind of message? Or tell you anything? Or tell you the truth? That someone wants to fuck you up? Manipulate you. Exploit you. Not communicate. OK. That's communication too. You're right. 'I want to fuck you up.' That's a message. But I don't want to fuck you up again and again, not even once. Kiki's called Kiki, and Miki Miki. Why? What a stupid, stupid question! I don't want to answer such a stupid, meaningless question. Why am I called Tonka? Get it? What a stupid question! In fact I shouldn't give a damn about what you think of me. But I do. I want to tell you my story somehow, but I wouldn't want you to see me as a menopausal idiot in her fifties . . . *There*, you see. I'm past fifty, but . . . OK. I'd like you to hear my story, but not to think that it's all because of the war. I used to be different. And then the war came and I went nuts. Lots of people went nuts, including me. PTSD. Post-Traumatic Stress Disorder. Come on. To get a 'post' trauma, you first have to have the trauma. Come on. I'll tell you my story. And you can think what you like, but if my story is a trauma, yours is too. I've thought a lot about this. What's the point of leaving Kiki? What's Kiki done to me? Why couldn't I forgive him? What couldn't I overlook? But does someone have to batter me, gouge my eye out with a fork, put out cigarettes in my cunt for me to leave him? Why couldn't I leave Kiki because he's good? Familiar. A book I already read. A village that wasn't destroyed. A river that flows murkily by. A bell on a bell tower that never goes wrong. Ivo Robíc and you're just seventeen. Why? Have you ever, you women who stay married, spent Sunday evening ironing while *he* was on the couch playing with the remote? You've got a backache, the children are outside, the electric bill's not paid, nor is the rent. He's fat or thin. Familiar. At first you're glad because the pile of un-ironed clothes is getting smaller. And then you stop. And with the iron in the air . . . Wait a minute! I'm forty! Or fifty! Or thirty, fuck it! I'll iron this pile, sit down and rest my back. And then shove the dishes into the dishwasher, take a shower and lie down beside this *thing*. I've lost interest. But this is my fate for the coming ten or twenty or thirty years. Has it ever occurred to you, you who stay with your husband, to press the hot iron into his face and, as he screams, to lock the door from the outside and go away? Forever! No? That's never occurred to you? You're lying, lying, lying bitches! What lying bitches! Who am I talking to? Who are you? All right. OK. Why are you lying? Do you think you'll be in any less of a coma if you lie? If you've fooled yourself, you've fooled the whole world? As though the world cares about your problems! The world doesn't give a fuck about your pile of un-ironed clothes and the moron you're going to spend the rest of your life with! But this, this thing you're living . . . This is life? And I'm a slut, am I? I'm a slut because tomorrow morning, at exactly seven o'clock, I'll be taking Miki by the balls and leaving? That's why I'm a slut while you're saints? Have you ever waited for your five-year-old child to say: 'I won't.' Mommy's Darling. That's what you call the thing. And you nearly sent his head flying across the room with a slap. Blood gushed out of his nose. And that calmed you down. Really calmed you. Because that was that. Whenever your mother phones you and starts talking in that little quiet voice like someone dying in a burning desert, you want to . . . Don't tell me, don't lie to me that you don't want to strangle her with your own hands. Why are you constantly figuring out how much a sick father costs you and how much you'd save if . . . Nurse, pads, medicine, treating his bedsores . . . Come on, you fucking liars! There's a difference between you and me. I'm leaving, you're staying. I'm not heartless. It's not easy to go. I've spent thirty years with my Kiki. OK. Maybe the war is to blame. Maybe all those stinking bodies on the screen and in the papers have shown me how little it takes to turn a twenty-year-old or forty-year-old or fifty-year-old body into a heap of maggots. I watch television all the time. For ten years I've been looking at people in masks. They drag dead bodies out of a pile or a grave or a pit. That's what it was like in the war. And now there's peace in Croatia. And they kill people in hospitals. Then they bury them quickly. And then they take them out of their grave or coffin in order to see how American dialysis machines killed them. Get it? I'm fucking tired of Croatian deaths. I'm afraid of death. It's all around me. I can smell it. Touch it. Feel it. See it. I'm afraid. That's why I'm leaving Kiki for Miki. Miki is young. Maybe he's farther away from death. You think I'm a slut. Sluts are smart. They always find some excuse for selling their pussies instead of . . . Instead of? Instead of? What? You don't sell your pussy? You married women who are stay? You give it away free? You're the Red Cross? Come on. The Red Cross doesn't hand out cunts. They hand out packages. Usually fewer packages than they should. Most of the packages are sold by Red Cross workers who pocket the money. But you, ladies, you don't come free either. You cook, iron, wash, fuck when you don't want to, prostitute yourselves to have the status of Married Women. You are Married Women. I'm a Married Woman too. But only a little longer. And then I'll be a Married Woman again. I understand you. You can't be a normal woman if you are not a Married Woman. You're right. But everything has its limits. My dear married friends, I'm fucking sick of it all.

For absolutely no reason I'm chewing on a 100 gram chocolate bar. And fiddling with the remote. A documentary. Some old people are telling their life stories. Maybe tonight is the Day of Liberation of Croatia? Or Refugee Day? Or some other important Day? I'm not turning on the sound, even though I like documentaries. They're the only shows I can stand. I also like shows based on true stories. When I read 'based on a true story,' that's it! I settle back on the couch, it might be three in the morning, I watch, wide awake, what people have gone through. I like it when a woman, suddenly, quite out of the blue . . . You know. She goes into the large firm where she works. An enormous lobby. People around her. Hurrying. Everyone to his elevator. She is a well-known lawyer or successful executive. Around fifty, but she looks like thirty-five because people don't like to watch women who are around fifty and who look as though they're around fifty. And she frowns. She touches her forehead with her slender hand, pale pink nails, and collapses as though she's been struck by lightning. I like lightning. And thunder. When it's pouring outside, and I'm in bed. Beside my Kiki's warm ass. That's what I like best. Yes. And then that woman collapses. Ambulance sirens, lights flashing. We're in a hospital. The hospital is great. Nurses slide quietly by. Have you ever been in one of our hospitals? Can you imagine going to our hospitals with a stroke? Or without one? Bare walls. You lie on a stretcher on the floor of the emergency room while the doctor shakes cigarette ashes in your eye. OK. Forget that. Let's go back to the woman. She's in the hospital. In a coma. Her children come. Grown-up. The daughter wears Armani, the son is younger. Her husband whispers sweet nothings into her comatose ear. Nothing stupid. In her coma, she must hear something like 'little horse.' Because he called her 'little horse' the first time he fucked her. Or the second. Anyway, the character whispers words that plunge deep into any woman's brain. And those are always words or a word that a man utters to a woman the first time he fucks her. We're expected to remember those words. But, my friend Nada (this is a little digression) forgot all those words. She told me:

-12-

'I don't remember a single word.' There are all kinds of people. There are a lot of oddballs. Yes. Six months and countless 'little horses' later, the woman wakes up. The end! Credits. Because in fact this is a series. I can't wait for the following Tuesday to see her first steps . . . eating through a straw . . . learning to speak . . . to write . . . A, B, C . . . Ten episodes. The end of the series. She's back in the enormous lobby. She touches her forehead lightly again, she frowns again . . . There! You tremble with fear! Another stroke! A second one! Even worse! Devastating? Shit! I love that crazy twist at the end of every true story! She is only tapping her forehead because she's forgotten *his* birthday. So she takes her cell phone out of her incredibly expensive handbag, a Louis Vuitton, and says: 'Little horse here . . .' Wild! I could have an orgasm over a story like that. Incredible, but based on a true event. And I like documentaries. The most ordinary ones. When large bucks fuck or clobber each other because of the females. I like it when a mother polar bear flees with her young from their father because he'd eat the young if he caught them. I like that white, lumbering race. Or when a stallion jumps on a mare and in the foreground you see his huge cock. Yes. That turns me on more than porn films where a black guy shows a tender, red-haired beautiful woman what has grown between his legs. I don't know why they always impale a fragile, red-haired woman with almost no pubic hair on some black guy's big dick. The contrast probably turns people on. He's enormous, she's fragile. He's black, she's white. Beauty and the Beast. People are morons. They believe anything. I don't like black men. Yes. I don't like black men. I don't like losers. Outsiders. People who have to smile. And be polite. I don't like the Serbs in Croatia either. When they say 'Babić,' they always add 'from Korčula.' But they're not from the island of Korčula. They're from the Dalmatian countryside. From some godforsaken hole where Babić is something different. OK. There are Croatian Babićes there too. But a Croatian Babić never explains things. And never adds 'from Korčula.' Croats think that it's self-evident that they are Croats. It is only the Serbs in Croatia who emphasize the fact that they are Croats. But they shit on the Serbs. How do I know? Well, now . . . because . . . because . . . I'm 'from Korčula.' OK. I said it. You can stick that fact up your ass. I said it. Blacks are fucked up. They've got nowhere to go. Wherever they show up there's trouble. No one likes them. They have thick lips and yellowish eyes . . . I'll tell you something. My friend was a soccer player when he was young. And those soccer players travelled from town to town by bus.

Then in the bus or in the locker room they all farted. We women never fart in a group. Men are different. Yes. Those soccer players farted and farted and farted and then a black guy joined the team. And he farted too.

'But,' said my friend, 'that really smelled. Enough to make you puke! What do those monkeys eat?'

And they made a rule that the black man couldn't fart. While they let rip. What was I going to say? Yes. Black men are black. You either like them, or you don't. OK. Presumably their mothers like them. But they're black too. They can't go around passing themselves off as white people. They can't add 'from Korčula' and turn white. Get it? But, if you're a Serb in Croatia, it's far worse than being black because you can add 'Korčula' and deceive decent people. You may get away with it. You may not. Then you'll be screwed. But you'll be screwed even if you get away with it. Sooner or later. Because you keep waiting for someone to discover that you've never fucking seen Korčula. That's trouble. And then again, some people are Serbs and feel like Serbs. They think it's normal to be a Serb. Mother's a Serb, Grandpa's lying in the Serbian cemetery in Benkovac with something written in Cyrillic on his headstone in the tall grass; they have their saints' days, their priests are hairy and they're allowed to marry . . . And when a little Serb is born, then he's called Alimpije or Sava or Tanasije. And that little male Serb and Leposava the little female Serb know that's what they are from birth. It's all clear. They may sometimes say 'from Korčula' but they know they're not. Get it? But me. My case. It's a mess. I'm not a Serb. But I have to add 'Korčula.' I'm not a Serb! I would most like, right now, to get up and yell into the darkness: 'I'm NOT a Serb!' But, who gives a shit? If they're Croats who don't care, I don't need to shout anything at their Croatian ears. If they do care, I'll never convince them. That's why blacks have it easier. You're black and who gives a shit? But this, white, but black. Screwed. OK. This is what happened. It was around 1950. I'm sure you don't care about the exact year, but every year that makes me seem younger is good. I can't come to terms with my age. It's not because of the war. It bothered me before too. My mother. She was a fighter in 1940 something. Probably not one but two or three. She spent the whole war in a bunker or near one. And she led some 'comrades' into the forest. Don't ask me why those people went into the damn forests. I don't know. I was never interested in her stories. I don't know anything about the Partisans. Or very little. I know that they were very thin and that they weren't allowed to steal or fuck. I know some did fuck anyway, that some people in those forests ate grass, while some other Partisans ate something meaty. I was told that by my mother's friend who spent years on Goli Otok. In '48 he asked why some Partisans ate and screwed. I don't like history. Or geography. If my life depended on whether I was able to show where Čazma was on a blank map, I'd be screwed. I don't know where fucking Čazma is. I don't know anything about any offensive, nor the name of a single national hero, nor a single secretary of SKOJ except for Lola. I know that Lola was young when he was killed and that he was a secretary. But I don't know whose secretary or of what. Of course I know about Comrade Tito. Unlike you, I saw him hundreds of times. My mother, my grandmother and I lived in Uvala, and Uvala is on the road down which Tito drove to his island of Brioni. I threw flowers at his Cadillac a lot of times and furiously waved a little paper flag. We children didn't experience that as some kind of great honor, an exciting thing, or history lesson. We little girls would put on little blue skirts, little white socks on our thin legs, white blouses on our bony shoulders, and wave until the procession disappeared round the corner. As soon as Tito went by, we'd change, climb onto the roof of the old restaurant and play doctor. I was always a doctor. With a short, thin stick I'd examine my little girlfriends' pussies or tickle the boys' little balls. Not one boy ever got an erection. Our tits were just beginning to grow then. Our little tits were funny. On the shore, against a hot wall, they'd slowly rise. In the sea they'd disappear. That's why we kept jumping in and getting out. And then there came a summer when we could no longer erase our tits with the cold water.

On the TV screen the old men are wiping away tears from their eyes. What has happened to them? I'm not going to turn on the sound. I shouldn't tell you this. But I'm going to. When he left for Ljubljana, Kiki kissed me and shoved five candy bars into the pocket of my bathrobe. 'Think of me until I get back.' At this moment I'm taking the second piece of the second candy bar out of its wrapper. My damn hands. I hate middle-aged women who can control themselves, who're thin as sticks at fifty something . . . Yes! Fifty something! Opatija. Government Housing Bureau. My mother's sitting at a wooden table of some kind. A comrade comes in. Tall. Dark. With a moustache. In uniform. That moustached master is in fact just helping another comrade. Someone who has to look at several Jewish apartments in Opatija, instead of someone else, some other comrade, because some comrade from the Central Committee is supposed to move to Opatija. And my mother has to show him the apartments. Let's go on. An Opatija villa. A nice apartment on some floor. The second. My mother raises the wooden blinds. The sea! Let's look at the apartment. Three large bedrooms, a living room, a bathroom, two balconies, high ceilings, big windows . . . Yes. The apartment is furnished. Pictures on the walls. Crystal chandeliers. My mother is wearing a skirt, a blouse, short cotton ankle socks and hob-nailed boots. Boots in summer? Why? Don't ask me. I've got a photograph. The comrade and my mother go into one of the bedrooms. The comrade throws my mother onto the bed. He takes off her underwear that Auntie Milka made for her. Flannel with little flowers on it. The comrade spreads my mother's legs and squirts me into her. My mother doesn't scream or ask any questions. The comrade gets off my mother, takes the crystal chandelier from the ceiling, and wraps it in a brown blanket. My mother wipes herself with the sheet. Jewish, silk. There's no water.

'This is for the comrade from the Central Committee,' said the comrade, pointing at the wrapped up chandelier. 'Bye,' said the comrade.

'Bye,' said my mother.

Four months later she waited for her period. In vain. Then she told her story to a male comrade. Yes, a man. Not a female comrade. The comrade went away to Karlovac, but Živorad Babić, not from Korčula, was a happily married man. But an honorable man. So he acknowledged me. In the entry in the register of births it says—name of father: Živorad Babić. My mother never told me any details. I only presume that Živko screwed my mother in a lovely Jewish apartment. I find that more acceptable than a fuck in an Opatija park or the secret service office. I never forgave my mother for having refused the Jewish apartment, even though she was given the choice. There weren't many like my mother. Wild about the Party. If a secret service officer hadn't fucked her in fifty something, she would have died a virgin. The Party was the world to her. She, my grandmother and I spent our lives in a basement. From that basement, I watched people's legs going by. Going up and down steps. Up down, up down. Some of the legs didn't come back because there was a road at the top of the steps. And some only went down because the road led to the shore. And we could have had a Jewish apartment! That's what my mother told me. With everything in it! Chandeliers, paintings, furniture, linen, crockery . . . Get it? We could just have moved in, and become human beings.

I hate poor people. They make me sick. I always thought I'd be rich. We are in fact rich, in a way. When my Kiki sells five or six stolen suits, then we get two thousand German marks. A person with money feels different. When you wear a Paloma Picasso round your neck, Bruno Magli on your feet, when you're tucked into a Barberi cashmere . . . somehow you're a different person. Once, during a blackout in the war, Kiki and I carried half-a-million marks across the border in our ancient Yugo car . . . It was like this. *Santa Barbara* was on television . . . And Aki adored *Santa Barbara*. And you know as well as I do that if you don't want a lot of shit at the border, then you have to drag a little kid along with you. Even customs men are only human. When they see a little kid in the car, or a packet of diapers or baby food . . . they're not the same people anymore. I'll tell it all from the beginning, so you'll understand. Once my Kiki had to get five-hundred-thousand marks over the border to his business partner. That's why we also put our Aki into our old Yugo, and she was hollering because of *Santa Barbara*. But we weren't sure Aki was enough. So Kiki bought a wreath at a flower shop and on the ribbon it said: 'With love to Auntie Jožica from Aki, Kiki and Tonka.' Get it? We're taking a wreath at around midnight to our relatives in Ilirska Bistrica. That's a village near the border. Stop yawning. Kiki had stuffed half-a-million marks into Aki's little pink Barbie doll suitcase. You think half-a-million marks is a mountain of money. It's not. The Croatian customs men simply waved us on. The Slovenes too. 'Where are you going?' 'Why are you travelling?' I just looked mournfully in front of me because of my late Auntie Jožica. We had a terrible quarrel because of that wreath. OK. I realize now that it was absurd. I remember, I said to Kiki when he appeared in the kitchen with the wreath in his hands:

'How could you have written "Love to Auntie . . ." on the ribbon, Kiki? White ribbon is only for children . . .'

'Don't talk nonsense,' said Kiki, 'they didn't have any mauve ribbon. It's wartime. All the ribbons have been used up. What does the color of the ribbon matter?'

'Kiki,' I said, 'you have to pay attention to every little thing when you're taking half-a-million marks over the border. The ribbon could fuck us up, Kiki. What if customs asks why you have written "Love to Auntie Jožica . . . ," obviously an older woman, on a white ribbon when white is for children and youth?'

I had said 'youth.' Strange word. I don't know why 'youth' should have occurred to me. Kiki went crazy. I'm sorry you don't know Kiki. He's a good man. And we love each other. We've been together for thirty years. I'm going to leave him tomorrow, but that doesn't mean I don't love him. People simply grow apart from one another. Oh, I see. You can't understand why I'm leaving Kiki. Yes. Kiki rarely gets mad. But, when he does get mad, oh boy! And that evening he really did! He threw things. He hurled the wreath with 'Love to Auntie Jožica' onto the kitchen floor. Kiki is normally pink. In the face I mean. That evening the blood vanished from his face. Disappeared. Suddenly my Kiki was white. 'Damn whore!' My Kiki never, never, never calls me a 'whore.' 'This is a fight for survival! This is a fight for life and death! Either we're crossing the fucking border or we're not. Why are you fucking around with me? Why are you dragging me into your darkness? Help me! Help me! You fucking cow!' Yes. Kiki started crying. He whimpered, full of sorrow. I hugged his head, he was sitting on the kitchen floor beside the wreath with the white ribbon. And I've already told you, whimpering. I was angry that he had called me a whore. But there are always extenuating circumstances. So I hugged Kiki's head again and said:

'Don't cry, don't cry, don't cry . . . It's just that I think the ribbon for an older person, for Auntie Jožica shouldn't be white . . .'

OK. You're not going to believe this. Kiki began laughing. Out loud. Really out loud. He shrieked.

He threw his head back and shrieked. I could see his crowns. And under the crowns, gold. He ought to change those crowns. Get porcelain ones. Three hundred marks a shot, that's a whole lot of money. But you shouldn't let yourself be taken for a ride. Don't let your dentist, the crook, put porcelain on both the upper and lower teeth. Because that destroys them. Grinding or chewing. But I don't know which.

'Pull yourself together, Tonka,' Kiki said to me.

What an expression 'pull yourself together'! That's just what he said.

'Auntie Jožica doesn't exist. She hasn't died. She never even lived. We have nothing to do with Auntie Jožica. And even if we had, Auntie Jožica wouldn't give a shit about the color of the ribbon. She's dead. Let's give it a rest. I'm tired.'

I was holding Kiki's head on my big tits, 40C, and stroking his curly hair.

'OK, Kiki,' I said. 'I agree. But, look at films. It's always the little things that screw the crooks. Always little things. They have great plans, and then they fuck up.'

'We haven't got great plans,' said Kiki. 'All I want, if you don't mess me up, is to transfer five-hundred-thousand marks to Slovenia. Then Željko will give us a car. That's all. Take the fucking cash over the border. That's not a great plan. The red Audi we'll get is worth five thousand marks. I'm not trying to make a million! In films it's the ones who play big-time who get fucked. What's a seven-year-old Audi? It's a stupid little job!'

I didn't say anything. So we got into our Yugo. And Aki sat in the back. And the Slovenes asked us, I've told you that, and then we got to Ilirska Bistrica, and went into an inn. We had a hard time finding a free table. Thirtieth of December. The Slovene pensioners were celebrating the New Year before the New Year. They were dancing polkas and laughing. And then a waiter brought in, on an enormous dish or a board, a fat roasted suckling pig with an apple in its mouth. The pensioners clapped. So did I. Aki was sleepy. Sipping a coke through a straw.

'Hey, Kiki,' I said, 'these guys haven't a clue that we could buy the whole inn and half the village.'

Kiki was tense. And then that guy came. Dark blue cashmere coat, dark grey Boss trousers, Boss shirt, Boss tie and church shoes. Classic. Apart from the shoes. Kiki handed him the Barbie suitcase. Aki yelled. He went out. Then came back. He gave Aki back the suitcase and stroked her face. Aki was sobbing. We got into the little Yugo. Kiki stopped at the border. Took the wreath out of the car, pulled off the ribbon with 'our love' on it and hurled it into the bushes. I don't know how to explain this. I felt bad. Why didn't Kiki feel the least respect for my late Auntie Jožica? That wreath was after all a sign of love. OK, the ribbon was wrong. But I couldn't bear the fact that he had thrown the wreath into the first dark bush he came to. What if someone had crapped in that bush? People always feel like crapping or peeing at the border. From fear, stress, panic. And that hurt me. Auntie Jožica's wreath was lying next to a turd, a shitty diaper or a pile of plastic bags. That hurt me.

On the TV the old people are crying. I have the sound off, but I see their red eyes. They wipe their noses and eyes. Old people never use tissue. And when they go to the market, they always stop at the stall selling under-pants from Turkey, vests, and big linen handkerchiefs. My mother has hundreds of handkerchiefs, but I always buy her handkerchiefs for her birthday. My friend, my best friend Ela, thinks that's wrong. Handkerchiefs are for crying. These old people are crying again. I press the remote. Our City channel. Why do only thin women walk along the Corso? Young girls. Where am *I*? Why doesn't anyone ever stop me on the Corso? Why don't they film *me*? Prejudiced pricks.

It's an unbelievable change, moving from a little Yugo into an Audi. A big red Audi 100, an '88. I can't drive. Of course I've taken the test. But I can't drive. Whenever I'm at the wheel, there's always trouble. When Aki was little—she told me this when she got older—she was really happy when I drove her to nursery school. 'Everyone honked at us and I put my tongue out at them.' I didn't know that then. I know that they honked. I remember that. Idiots. Jerks. Shitheads. Always rushing. I didn't want to take my driving test. 1978. Kiki insisted. You must, you must, you must. OK. I don't like fighting over little things. Or even over big things. So I signed up for lessons. I didn't understand anything. I'm probably stupid. I studied for the fucking tests but I didn't get any of it. What do you do if you see a rock in the middle of the road? Move it? Leave it? Kick it? Circle the correct answer! Fucking tests. And fucking geometry in high school. Kiki must have paid off someone, because I passed the written test. And the driving one. I always break into a cold sweat when I drive. And I'm always surprised that people think it's fine when they see me at the wheel. Lots of people drive. Everyone drives. But I know that it isn't fine for me to drive. It's crazy. Yesterday I was at a roundabout, and was supposed to turn from one lane into another after stopping first, because the people in the other lane had the right-of-way. I didn't stop. And I didn't look. A man slammed on his brakes. But he still ran into our red '88. Yes. He ran into me. On my side. My left arm hurts. That's why I'm holding the remote in my right hand. Even though I'm left-handed.

Those old people are crying again. Then taking out their handkerchiefs. I find that strange. You wipe your nose on a big handkerchief, then you spread it out and look at what's in it. I don't like people who waste time looking at what comes out of them. My Kiki is obsessed with his shit. Is it black, light, dark? Then he asks me what that means. I rarely read the *Home Medicine* book so I don't know. I do know that if you shit black it's cancer, but it could also be beetroot, blueberries or red wine. We hardly ever buy blueberries because they're expensive. I used to eat them years ago. When my blood iron was two. Blood iron of two! That's a coma. You're dead. It could have been leukaemia or cancer or some other shit. So I was in the hospital. I'm horribly, horribly, horribly afraid of doctors and death. I always imagine that the doctor will say: 'Sit down, madam,' and look at me with a solemn expression. OK. I know that this solemn doctor is going to croak too. That he's solemn although he doesn't give a shit about me. That I wouldn't give a shit about him either if I had to look at him solemnly. But that doesn't do me any good. When my blood iron was two, it was a Friday. I was supposed to go to the hospital on Monday. I bought blueberry juice, and I drank red wine and took iron tablets. And I got diarrhea. Black. I sat on the heater and shivered. People shiver when they have leukemia or cancer. I was shivering so hard that I couldn't keep my mouth closed. I don't know why I wanted to have my mouth closed. Why was I bothered by my mouth being open? I held my mouth with my hand. And shivered. And cried. And cried. And cried. I hate the thought that I'm going to die. And that others will be left. I don't think it's my time to die yet. I like going to the duty-free shop, buying Paloma Picasso, I want to get divorced, marry Miki the lawyer. He'll come for me tomorrow morning at seven. And I'll grab him by the balls. I've already told you that. And then Kiki took me to the emergency room.

'Lie down,' said a young doctor and injected me in the ass with a sedative.

I find it very difficult to fall asleep. That's because of menopause. Or the war. I don't sleep at all. And now I'm looking at the TV screen. I told you about those old people. Now I'm on the City channel. Elections. Tents on the Corso. Local politicians invite people to talk to them in their tents. Fuck them! I never vote. I don't give a shit about politics. With the sedative in my ass I slept, and slept, and slept. In the hospital, the leader of the team asked me:

'How many pads do you use when you menstruate, madam?'

What a stupid question.

'I don't know,' I said.

'Take iron tablets and eat horse meat.'

I love horses. But not as meat. Horses for me are not horse meat. But I didn't tell the old fucker that. I was in a ward with four women. One had a huge belly. She wasn't pregnant. She had cirrhosis. In fact she was dying. And every morning the physiotherapist got her up and walked around the ward with her. The woman dragged her feet.

'We never give up hope,' said the woman doctor, 'that's why they do exercises. There's always hope.' Hope? Hope for a yellow, rotten, tired body? And then that woman asked for Neurofen. They didn't have any. Panadol. There wasn't any. Aspirin. Nor that. She screamed with pain. The whole day. And night. You don't have to believe me. At three in the morning I called a taxi and went home. I rang the bell somewhat timidly. I'm not usually timid. I believe in myself. My tits still look good, because I'm not scrawny. My hair is always dyed, I never have grey roots, and my teeth are in good shape. And if you always have a big smile, you look ten years younger. Read *Mila* magazine. But nevertheless, that night I was timid. What if Kiki's not alone in our bed? What if he's written me off? What if I have cancer and no one's telling me? My palms were sweating, I trembled in front of my own front door. I waited. And rang the bell. And rang. Kiki sleeps soundly. Aki opened the door for me. I told her about the lady with cirrhosis. And fell into bed. Let me die at home. I snuggled up to Kiki. I took him by his little cock and fell asleep. It used to be that three green sleeping pills were enough to last for a night and half-a-day.

Shall I put on the sound so you can hear what the old people are saying? No. It's depressing. It might upset you. Maybe you don't like listening to sad stories at this time of night. What time of night? This. As though it matters whether it's two in the morning or five. I'm waiting for seven.

I told you. The guy ran into me from the left and that's why my left arm is hurting now. I do everything with my left hand. I only write with my right. When I write. But I never write. Who to? Then that man got out of his car, I don't know what kind, I don't know anything about cars.

'Are you crazy?! Are you out of your mind? You could have killed yourself and me!'

I told you I hate arguments, shouting and quarrelling. I never quarrel. So I just looked at him.

'Why don't you say something? Who gave you your license?'

I said: 'Matulji district, in 1978. That's where I took the test, but there's no driving school there anymore. In that building. Now they sell refrigerators there. Bosch. I wouldn't have known that, but we recently bought a big Bosch there with a credit card, so I know. I don't know what the interest rate is though . . .'

The man looked at me.

'Are you insane, lady? Are you drunk?'

I never drink. And why should I be insane? People always think you're insane if you answer their questions. He had asked me, 'Who gave you your licence?' I replied 'Matulji district.' What's insane about that? Was I supposed to say nothing? Call my lawyer? Shout at the man, tell him to go to hell? Confess? 'It's my fault.' But he hadn't asked me whether it was my fault. He asked me who gave me my license. The police came. We had to take a breath test. I told you I never drink. They took our cars away. I'm leaving my Kiki tomorrow. And what will I miss? Our old, red '88 Audi. I didn't tell you the main thing. Why I love that car. When I drive it no one honks at me. I can crawl along the road, people see I'm a woman, but they don't honk. Get it? But when I was in the Yugo everyone honked. It was like being in a wedding procession. And I always saw mean faces in my rearview mirror. Scowling. Furious. I'll tell you the important thing because I don't like screwing around for a long time. In the Audi I felt rich and successful and big. Sitting in the Audi, I deflected attention from myself. I hate, hate, hate people looking at me. Noticing me. Honking at me. When people look at me, I go berserk. And I don't like answering questions. It really gets to me. A lot. The war? Was it the war? OK. The war. I don't expect the state to pay me any money because I'm troubled. But I am troubled. For good reason, however. Now you're going to say I'm a pathetic, over-sensitive bitch who doesn't understand the war and what they did to us. I get it. 'What they did to us.' But I don't give a shit about us. What they did to *me*. Me! Me! Me! That father of mine, that Serbian piece of garbage who squirted me out in '50 something . . . Yes, '50 something! Yes! Why did he acknowledge me? My mother didn't care. Getting fucked wasn't traumatic for her. Being pregnant was fine with her, she got some coupons for me, oil, sugar, and fifty square meters of linen for diapers. She didn't miss love. However idiotic it sounds to you and me, she loved the Party. I was a gift from the Party. Through a delegate. I tried, I tried a thousand times to find out why my mother hadn't asked the Party for something else. In vain. 'That's not what I fought for.' 'That?' What's 'that' you didn't fight for, you crazy cow? And what did you fight for? My mother would die of hunger today if Kiki didn't sell a suit or a tie. 'That's why I sleep peacefully.' Really? But I don't sleep peacefully, Mother! Why have you fucked up my sleep? Why did fucking Živko acknowledge me? 'That's the way things were then.' Fuck 'then,' Mother! Fuck 'then,' Mom . . . I'll tell you how I got my Croatian residence permit.

I looked into those eyes. Into the eyes of that woman. Ordinary eyes. Brown. Tired. Cloudy. Like yours.

'Where was Živorad Babić . . . ?' she yelled.

'Živko,' I said, 'Živko . . .'

'Where was Živorad Babić in '47 . . . ?'

'But, what does it matter . . . ?' I asked.

'Get out,' screamed the woman, 'out!'

I left the room. There were two policemen outside the door, they hadn't been there when I went in, and the line of people waiting stretched as far as Belgrade Square, which isn't called that anymore. I had fought my way through all those Muslims, Albanians, Bosnians and Serbs who pretended to be Croats and I could hardly wait to get out. Think whatever you like

-34-

about me! I'm not a Serb! I'm not a Serb! I'm not a Serb! Fuck fucking Živko Babić! People started giving me a lot of room. And sniffing. I realized I had soiled myself. Had crapped. I went into the toilet and took off my panties, and looked at the crap. A dark, almost black turd. I felt (you don't have to believe me) a kind of joy. There, look what you've done to me! I've got cancer! I've got colon cancer! It'll be on your conscience, lady! Of course the filthy cow doesn't have a conscience. It's obvious she's a Serb! There's no Croat who isn't a Serb! A lot her Serbian cunt cares about my Serbian ass. She's just protecting herself. But I felt somehow righteous. Important. I was a completely innocent victim. And then I remembered that Kiki had exchanged six ties for a kilo of blueberries. Boro, that Boro from the market, was going to a wedding and he needed those ties. I realized that the black turd was not divine justice but too many blueberries on an empty stomach. Kiki gave the bitch a thousand marks and I got my residence permit. I hear you asking whether I paid off the apartment. Yes. So why the hell are you complaining? And what did they do to us? That's the way things were then. But I was fired. That's what I'm telling you. You were fired too. We were all fired! OK. But you weren't fired because you were fucking Serbs. You were fired for the usual reasons. Because times were hard. You're not black. You're white. But things don't always work out for whites either. That's how it is. I'd be glad if I'd been fired as a lazy white bitch. Or because you're not needed anymore. Maybe you're right. Whose fault is it if my mother screwed the first Živko who took his secret service prick out in front of her? In '50 something. Yes! Fifty something! There. If my mother hadn't been a Serbian slut then I wouldn't be a Babić from the countryside but a Babić from Korčula. OK. You're right. But, if my mother had screwed a Babić from Korčula, I wouldn't be here. I've thought about it all. And that's the fucking catch. The fucking dilemma! Fucking shit! Either you're a Serb or you don't exist. Get it? Of course you do. You're not idiots. But you're not Serbs, so you don't give a shit. And you don't care about how it was for me. I've got a best friend. Ela. She has stayed with me. What a feeling! You sit in the office. And no one calls you. The telephone never rings for you. You're alone. And naked. Like a French whore who hung around with Germans for the whole war and so they'll shave her head. They haven't yet, but they will. You're a whore with a full head of hair, but not for long. Ela called me every day. She acted as though she thought this would all end one day. As though Živko were an in-fected bladder or flu. You have to keep warm or drink willow-herb tea. Then Živko will disappear. But what did they do to us? There you go again. OK, so they messed you up too. They fucked you up. OK! OK! OK! Are you going to inform on me? Are you going to kill me? I'm a Chetnik? A Chetnik slut! But Kiki's not a Chetnik! He's a Croat! Miki's a Croat too! I've never been fucked by a Serb! Only Croats! Fuck you, Chetniks! Why are you upsetting me? What's your problem? I'm lying peacefully in bed, the old people on the screen are wiping their noses with big handkerchiefs and crying. The night is warm or cold or wet or windy. I'm holding the remote in my right hand and telling my story. Why are you pissed off? I'm pissed off? Me? That's what you think? But you're the majority, and I'm the minority. That's why you think I ought to loosen up and be less sensitive. I think that there aren't many of us left, us Babićes who are not from Korčula, and that people should stop fucking us up. Our problem has been solved. 'Ours'! There, you see what you've done to me! I've become *us*! I've become *us*! *Our* problem! Why the fuck is it *our* problem? I'm me! Me! I'm me! Someone wrote with spray paint on the door of our apartment, 'Get out of Croatia!' Me? Who doesn't know geography and has never lived 'outside'! The neighbors stopped greeting me. And Mihajlo who lives in our building and has a butcher shop on the ground floor became Miroslav and a fucking Croat overnight. And he didn't want to sell me half a chicken, and at that time there wasn't a Bila megamarket in the city.

'I don't want problems because of you, Tonka.'

Serbian trash! Suddenly I was 'Tonka' with no 'Mrs.' We moved in with Ela. I was afraid they'd cut my throat if I stayed at home. Every evening I shoved the old boiler up against the front door. And a big table. Kiki was against that.

'Why are you so paranoid?'

I'd spend the whole night listening for footsteps on the stairs of our building.

'I don't want them to catch me off guard! I want to fight! I don't want to die like a stupid Jew!'

'Remember,' said Kiki, 'you're not goddamn Anne Frank. They don't give a shit about you. You don't mean anything! If they killed off everyone the Serbs had screwed throughout Croatia, there wouldn't be any women left in this country.'

That was vicious. The liar! I don't know many women like me. Nor many mothers like my mother. The way Kiki talks it sounds as though all Croatian women are Serbian sluts. But that's not true. OK. I'm not saying that my mother was a slut or a Serbian slut. But I can't forgive that Živko of hers. I can't and I won't. That year, don't ask me which, I started calling people named Babić from Korčula. 'Hello, I'm Tonka, Tonka Babić from Korčula . . . I don't have a father, I'm looking for my roots . . . If you can . . .' People hung up the phone on me. There were warships around Korčula. And right under my window too. A lot the Babićes from Korčula cared about Tonka Babić whose accent told them she was not from the island. I didn't sleep at night. And during the day I protested with the Rampart of Love organization in front of the military headquarters of the city. We, women and men, yelled, trying to get our fucking kids out of the notorious Yugoslav People's Army. To give them what they fucking deserved. To beat them! At that time, if I'd been able to, I would have broken every young soldier's thin Yugoslav neck with my bare hands. I would have strangled them, lifted up the corpse and said, in the middle of the Corso: 'Look! Look what a Babić from Korčula can do!' The fucking kids didn't come out of the army. And that day I almost shit in my pants. We yelled so loudly. All our eyes were rolling, our mouths wide open and big and wide. We stood pressed up against one another. You could smell the stench from the mouths of smokers and those who never brushed their teeth and the diabetics. Diabetics have a particular smell. So, we yelled. And then the face of a fine gentleman was pushed into my face. I smelled Gautier. I know Gautier well. That's what Kiki smells of.

'I know you,' snarled Gautier.

I was really afraid. Like I had never been before in my life. What if he grabs me by the throat? Where will I run to? My hands became damp and icy. My mouth dry. Yes. My whole life flashed before my eyes. Diving into the water in the bay, my grandmother eating apples, with little pieces passing down her thin neck, meeting Kiki on Slatina when I fell and scratched my knee and tore my net stockings. Him fucking me on the beach in Opatija, the first time, and I shrieked. He thought that it was wild passion but I had a piece of broken beer bottle in my ass. Lying on the warm sand on my stomach, while Kiki took the glass out of my ass. I forgot what my first fuck was like because my impressions got mixed up with that piece of beer bottle. My Aki going to school. And she didn't want to go into the classroom although she was seven and a half and she was the only one who cried. So I went in with her. And on every bench there was a bunch of wild flowers. For those little children. And I cried and cried and cried. And then I remembered that I had never hugged my mother. That I ought to have hugged her, despite everything, and kissed her. Before death. Mine. And it occurred to me that I loved Kiki, but that

I hadn't told him so for years. And I wanted to say to all those kids from the Headquarters: kids, don't be afraid, I'm not going to break your Yugoslav necks, and I remembered that I had left the house in a black bra and white panties with torn, black pantyhose under my slacks. And at the autopsy they'd undress me and say, look at the fucking Serb, she doesn't have a white bra . . .

'You don't know me,' I said.

'I do,' said Gautier cheerfully, 'you're my son's girlfriend's mother.'

'No I'm not,' I said cheerfully, 'I'm your son's girl-friend.'

And we laughed. And then shouted again.

Where was I? Oh yes. I felt unsafe. So we moved in with Ela. Aki went to stay with my mother at the bay. My mother never had problems with being a Chetnik slut during the war. How strange. Nor did Aki. Only me. Ela was a sub-tenant in the Hills. Those are badly built apartments. Prefabricated. Thin walls. I don't know how to describe them. In those days all young married couples had the same three-seater sofas like wooden buckets. Beige-colored. They looked young and hip. But it was impossible to sleep on them. Nevertheless, Kiki and I lay down on the pull-out sofa. I felt safe at Ela's. Don't ask me why. I don't know. I didn't take any pills at night or listen to footsteps on their stairs. But I did listen to Ela and Boris fucking. Every night. Boris grunted. He made noises like a wild boar. I presume that's what a wild boar sounds like. Not that I'm a goddamn hunter. Who'd know. I don't walk around forests and I don't record the sounds of wild boar. And I don't pick mushrooms like my friend who's afraid of bears and calls her husband every five seconds with a whistle. And he goes berserk. Because he hates whistles and because he's not afraid of bears. Ela made high, throaty noises. Like a bird with a noose around one thin little leg. If that's the noise birds make when they're in such a mess. And then she'd whisper: 'Quiet, quiet . . .' And then again the wild boar grunting and the bird with its little leg in a noose . . . One night I grabbed Kiki by the cock. He respected the state of mind I was in and left me in peace. 'I don't want to rape you,' Kiki told me. So one night I grabbed him by the cock. And we screwed. I didn't come, but I yelled. For the hell of it. Let a Serbian yell rend the Croatian air. What a stupid, stupid, stupid cow.

When did I meet Miki? How? Where? Does he know how to fuck? How did it come about, me at my age and him twelve years younger? Is he married? Children? He's not a faggot? Where will you live . . . ?

What questions. What banal, stupid questions. How would it be if I asked *you*? Are you unfaithful to your husband? Does your mistress have orgasms? Why do your grown-up children pee in bed? Why is your daughter a slut? How can you not know when everyone else knows? Why do you pay five hundred marks for each of your son's exams? Why are you screwing your wife's best friend? Why do you lie that you're a Croat when you're a fucking Muslim? And you got your residence permit only after that fat Istrian drunken priest baptized you for a thousand marks plus lunch in his brother's restaurant. And you became Hadžiselimović the Croat. Crap. Crap. Crap. Why do you like poking around in other people's lives? Why don't you straighten out your own fucking little life? Inquisitive shits! But you don't give a fuck! I'm in a good mood tonight. I'll answer all your questions. These old people on the TV. This is crazy. The journalist holds the microphone under their noses and she even cries discreetly. So that the camera picks up her tears in the foreground. The slut. The big lying whore. Crying. For the sake of the program. And she has so much make-up on that her tears just run over it. But nothing happens. Her eyes aren't red. They're beautiful. And shining. Her sadness is subtle. Refined. Polite. Croatian sadness. When I see that kind of bitch,

I'm really glad I'm a Serb. That kind of snivelling Croat. And then it occurs to me that the bitch may be a Serb or some other foreign shit, and I feel better. The slut is only earning her lousy living. Journalists. You think journalists are heroes. They've told the truth. They've photographed a lot of frontlines. Many of them died. They've changed a lot of things. If there were no journalists, we'd all still be . . . Go on, stupid morons! What would it be like here if there were no journalists? What would my life be like if there weren't any? I'll tell you, you stupid assholes: the same! The same! I can swear to you by my father Živorad's Serbian prick that journalists never change anything! For the better I mean. Never! Nothing! You think I ought to keep quiet! That I ought never to say such a thing! Journalists are powerful! Vain! They have influence! You have to be careful with them! Smile! And how will they get to know what I think about them? How? It's the middle of the night. This is just between you and me. You're not going to go around telling everyone. You won't tell anyone? I'd be glad if you didn't. I'd be glad if you were heads without tongues. That's what Dalmatians call people who don't go around telling everything. People who know how to keep a secret. They call them 'heads without tongues.' What a good expression! It's really good! Good, good, good! OK.

You'll say that I'm a 'tongue without a head.' Good. I like that, a 'tongue without a head.' I think that's great. Great! I've got my opinion about journalists. I know that they're just shits. But I don't have the guts to stand in Ban Jelačić Square and shout about it. I don't have the balls. Journalists! Cheap shits. This country is totally fucked. Blackest of black nights. Hunger, chaos. You think that's because of the war? Like hell it's because of the war. You're sure that what flared up was the long cocooned fifty-year hatred between Serbs and Croats? Good word, 'cocooned'! Good! And you swallow that story about cocooned hatred! I'm a Serb and I've spent fifty years hating you, Croatian garbage, and now I've come into my own? But in the wrong place. I'm the aggressor, but an aggressor who hasn't a chance because I'm surrounded by civilized philanthropists. If I were in Belgrade, I'd eat Croatian meat without horseradish! Because horseradish gives me hemorrhoids. OK, you're not a shit. In fact you don't give a flying fuck who impregnated my mother. Serbian Živko or Croatian Ante. Journalists told you who I am. But journalists don't give a damn about me either. They aren't people who think about me at all. Or people who make mistakes. Or people who think the wrong thing. They are mercenaries. Whatever their master tells them, that's their truth.

Journalists don't have money. And if they had their own money, car, apartment, house, yacht, they'd mortgage everything and spread the truth. The hell they would. Are you following me, you manipulated shitheads? Someone pays those guys. To make trouble and create panic. And then you turn on me. And you hate me although I'm good, although I never, never, never, never saw that damn, fucking Živko! Fuck him! Fuck my grandmother Živadinka! Gran! Nan! Nanny Živadinka! Gran is my mother's mother. There! You see! Journalists! Journalists in Croatia! Every newspaper in Croatia has its owner. And its sacred cows. There's no way journalists from *Istok* would ever say that a politician had raped a five-year-old child, if that trash was their sacred cow. But they'll cheerfully publish the fact that the little girl was raped by someone else, a beast from the neighbouring cage, although she wasn't. Get it? Those guys lie when they feel like it. This bitch, the one on the screen. What in hell is she crying for? Because these quivering old people lost everything in the war? As though she gives a rat's ass about the war. If it hadn't been for the war her blunt snout wouldn't have become an editor's snout. In wartime, when there's a lot going on, the bosses have to go looking for stupid snouts with big eyes full of fat tears. And find them. Overnight. So that pretty mouths can talk a lot of crap. I don't buy that story. This fat bitch can turn on the tears. She can pour her pretty eyes out between her bare legs. I don't give a shit. I don't believe a word she says. And I won't turn on the sound. Cry, you slut, without me! You don't understand, do you! You think I'm exaggerating. My little car accident this morning has shaken me up? You're crazy! That's not the first accident in my life. The car hit me from the side and fucked up my left arm, not my head. OK. You don't get it? Let's take it slowly. Look at those Americans. All the papers are full of them. They're on TV screens all over the world. The whole world is talking about the wretched Taliban women. How they feel under that cloth they wear. With little slippers on their feet. The whole, whole, whole world is talking about it. About the Americans going to war to take the Taliban women's headwear and slippers off. So that the Taliban women can walk freely and stomp loudly with thick heels. Buy that crap if you want. My Serbian heart, which I don't have, really bleeds. The way the journalists write about it, it turns out that the Americans are freedom fighters. Where the hell is freedom here? They come and pull freedom out of their asses. Come on! OK, let's take it slowly, so you understand it all. Bin Laden destroyed their twin towers. You can imagine. But that's what they sell us. The Americans have the CIA, they have the FBI, they have satellites, they have everything under the sun. If I were to fart now, although I don't fart in bed, unless I'm certain that Kiki is sleeping soundly and then I fart quietly and lift up the covers, to air out the bed. All right . . . But let's say that I fart now. The fucking Americans would register it somewhere. Somewhere it would say 'Tonka,' daughter of I-hope-the-late Živko Babić, son of that bitch Živka, if she was called Živka, or maybe she still is, 'farted at . . .' Then they'd write down the time. Get it? And they didn't know about the attack on the fucking Trade Center? They didn't know???! Like hell! Why are you breathing deeply? Why are you groaning? You're idiots! Manipulated! You believe the newspapers! Yes! Inhale! Yes! I'm telling you that the Americans sacrificed several thousand of their citizens so they could attack the Taliban trash. Whether it's oil or some other crap they're after, I don't know. But it's not a battle for the freedom of some oppressed women, I'm sure of that. You're surprised the Americans sacrificed their own people. Americans? Yes indeed, ladies and gentlemen! So whose lives should they sacrifice? Hungarians? Whose people do politicians sacrifice to get their stupid nation on its feet? Their own. Who aren't 'theirs' in any way. They're just people. A nation.

Cattle. Cannon-fodder and grenade launchers and Boeings without an American pilot. Three thousand Americans went to see their Maker. The others went berserk. And the politicians restricted all the rights of those others and sent thousands of them to hell to take chadors off the Taliban women. Get it? No, you don't get a damn thing. I wouldn't either if my father wasn't called Živko. If my father was Hrvoje, I wouldn't get it. And I wouldn't smell a victim. Only victims smell victims. I'm not a victim? So what did they do? I'll tell you again, leave me alone. What on earth do I have to do with 'them'? What on earth do the Taliban women have to do with the Americans? Nothing, but in fact they do. I, daughter of the I-hope-late Živko, and a fucked-up Taliban woman with headwear, we're the same. So is the American who takes little slippers off Taliban women's little feet in the middle of nowhere. Someone is playing a game in our name. The chador is being removed for our good. But, my blind friends, what you don't get is that we're all under the chador. The fucking Taliban women are under the chador. The deceased Americans from the twin towers are under the chador, so are the living Americans in godforsaken Indiana and Afghanistan and Iraq and Iran and Bosnia-Herzegovina and Guatemala and the Philippines and in Italy. I'm under the chador, and so are you assholes who don't understand a fucking thing. Is there anyone who's not covered, I hear you yelling full of hope. There are. In the world there are perhaps a hundred or a hundred and fifty sons of bitches whose heads aren't covered and who hold our lives in their hands. The entire world is being fucked by five corporations, ones like Coca-Cola. The rest of us are Taliban women.

I'm slowly losing the thread. What did you ask me? When was the first time Miki screwed me? And when did you screw the first time? How was it? You've forgotten. I'll tell you. It was nothing special. She probably didn't have an orgasm. She certainly didn't if *you* were screwing her. OK. OK. Don't get pissed. That was meant to be a joke. The first time? I'd pass over that first time. But then, why? The night is long. Seven o'clock is far away. Or maybe it's not. It's fun not telling you what time it is. It really amuses me. And now you don't know whether I'm going to grab Miki by the balls in half an hour or six hours. Great. A good feeling. I've eaten all the candy bars. Five of them. If you knew how long it takes me to eat one bar, multiplied by five, you'd know what time it is. Yes! But you don't know when I began. Ha! The first time? I went to Miki's with Ela. You remember Ela, my best friend. We went to his office together. Miki is the best lawyer in the city. For divorces. Not all lawyers are good for everything. The ones who are great at divorces haven't a clue about criminal cases. They wouldn't be able to defend a murderer even if you fucked them. But they can extract the last kuna from a husband. And the other way around. Some can get a murderer out on bail after three days, but they're not capable of getting three kunas out of a husband. But they can get a heap of kunas from the murderer's relatives. While the guy's in jail. As soon as he comes out, it's a bit more difficult. Even the worst murderer thinks he's innocent as soon as he's out. I can't be bothered to tell you why Ela went into Miki's office and why I had to stay in the waiting room. I don't like spreading around other people's dirty little secrets. I'm not going to tell you anything. I'm a head without a tongue. When Ela and Miki came out of his office I looked at Miki. I don't know how old your husband is. Maybe thirty or maybe sixty. Kiki's . . . All right. I get it. You're not interested in Kiki. Or me. But Miki. His office is on the Corso. This isn't right. I'm jumping from Ela to Miki from Miki to Kiki from Kiki to the office . . . Let's take it slowly. What does Miki look like? Lawyers are all the same, in a way. Dark or light, expensive suit, Canali, Zenya, Boss or something like that, stolen. Light-colored shirt, bought. Silk tie, stolen. Pacciotti shoes, stolen. Expensive bridge briefcase, about a thousand marks or more, bought. Clean-shaven. Expensive cologne, Armani or Boss or . . . bought. And that's it. That's Miki. And young. If you take twelve years away from my age, that'd be it. But you don't know how old I am! Ha! Ha again! His office is colorful. That would be the word. Pictures on the walls. Botero. Reproductions, obviously. What are you thinking of! Botero is possibly the most expensive living painter. How do I know? Read *Gloria* magazine. Then Vojo Radoičić, Damir Stojnić, those are originals, then . . . But you're not interested in that. And he has a big leather armchair in his office. There are ordinary chairs in the waiting room. Grey. Actually, the armchair looks like leather, but it's not. How do I know? I know the smell of leather. So, he's got a leather armchair made of good imitation leather, I ought to have left out that 'leather' and just said 'good imitation leather,' because if it's good imitation then it's not leather . . . Your nitpicking is getting on my nerves. If I have to pay attention to every word, if you correct me, I'll go mad. Then I won't tell you about our first fuck. Miki has a picture of his wife and daughter on his desk. His wife is young. Thin, long honey-colored hair. Shoulder-length. The little girl has white hair. That's called 'baby-blonde.' I was blonde once. Real baby-blonde. I wanted to be baby-blonde. The hairdresser assured me that I was baby-blonde. And then I was at the funeral of the secretary of the managing director of Jadroplov. That's where I worked. I was crying in the third row of the funeral. Some type behind me said to some other type: 'I'd screw that yellow one.' He said 'yellow.' And he meant me. So I figured out that I was not baby-blonde, that the hairdresser had screwed me, so I changed both my hairdresser and my hair color. Now I go to Alexandra. But Miki's little girl is baby-blonde.

I can't say I've read many books. I'm not saying that. I can't say that I read every *Women's World*, *Life*, *Gloria*, *My Secret*, *My Sorrow*, *My Story*. I do read. And I read love stories. All the bullshit fucking comes at the end of long suffering, doubt, soul-searching. 'Soul-searching,' what a good word! In a love story the wife of the main character is a bitch, and the girl who wants to screw the main character is a virgin. Before the end of the story the bitch is killed in a car crash, opening the way for the virgin to the bastard's heart. Oh yes, the bastard has a little daughter with baby-blonde hair, a blonde baby, and even before her mother—the bitch—is killed, the little girl with baby-blonde hair preferred that servant or nanny or companion (I like the word 'companion') to her slut of a mother. So they bury the whore, they put the child into her little bed, the girlfriend reads her the story about the seven kids without the wolf because the child has just lost her mother, such as she was, she was still her mother, so the wolf was left out so that the child didn't have to have another shock, and then that servant and the son-of-a-bitch father (who owns half the village and two multinational companies) drink dry sherry by the fire, he a glassful, she just a drop because in addition to being a virgin, she doesn't drink. There's sadness around them because they've just come back from a funeral, the funeral of a slut but still a funeral, but one can sense, it's in the air, that, once the sorrow over that slut passes, there's no real sorrow but because of people, because of the villagers, when even that kind of sorrow passes, one can sense that the two of them will fuck. There. That's how things are in the story supplements to *Gloria*, *Regina*, *My Sorrow*, *My Story* . . .

But, I'm not a companion and Miki isn't married to a slut. His wife is a normal human being who works in insurance and is never at home. That's a really demanding job, persuading people in this Croatian poverty to insure their little apartment, house or old refrigerator. We've got that straight. That young woman, Anna, is not a slut, I'm not a companion, while Miki the lawyer doesn't pay even his membership to the thieving lawyers' association because future divorcées don't have any cash before their divorce. Nor after it either, in fact. So Miki's not exactly rolling in money. We screwed like this. I once went to Miki's without Ela. Maybe I told you, and maybe I didn't. I go regularly to Alexandra, that's my hairdresser, my teeth are porcelain, I'm always laughing, I'm a cheerful woman, people like cheerful women, I talk a lot, people like people who are a tongue without a head and I have great underwear. Whenever he finds good underwear, Kiki first selects a bra and silk panties for me. That day my hair had just been dyed. I'd been to Alexandra the day before because a hairdo looks or falls better (don't be hung up on details) the following day. Black undies, a silk, tight teddy, black pantyhose, not thick, but thick enough so that my spider veins didn't show, and a black Yves Saint Laurent dress. You imagine, because you haven't a clue, that expensive dresses look glamorous. And that they can only be worn to opening nights or the President's birthday. Bullshit, ladies and gentlemen! It's sad to be poor and never to see an expensive dress. If you weren't poor, if you had dough, so that you could buy your wife a dress like the one I had on then, you would know that they can be worn at midday and midnight. And on the hanger it looks like the smock I used to wear to high school in Opatija. When? Then! The whole dress does up with one button. One single button. And I sparkled in that bra and teddy and pantyhose. Yes. I realized I'd screwed up. Kiki had got me a red garter belt for Christmas, and red underwear and red stockings and maybe it would have been better if I had put them on. More sexy. Sexier. But I didn't. That whole red combination might after all have been too shocking. I didn't want Miki to think I had prepared for it. I wanted taking my clothes off to look spontaneous. Like, suddenly my hormones had gone to my head. I'm going to admit something. Although I shouldn't. My hormones don't go to my head. Neither spontaneously nor intention-ally. I don't have any hormones anymore. Or I have them, but I'm not aware of them. I don't give a fuck about sex. What could I call that? What kind of figure of speech is that: 'I don't give a fuck about sex'? What kind of construction is that? That I don't give a fuck about sex, when what I mean is I don't feel like fucking at all. What a poet! So what in hell drove you to take off your clothes in front of someone else's husband and the father of an underage child with baby-blonde hair? I don't know. Get it? I don't know. It wasn't about wild love. Heated passion. The desire for a piece of young, sinewy, thin, hard, new flesh. Nothing like that. I just took off my clothes, and that's it. Without desire or any specific intention. Out of boredom or for the sake of a change or out of curiosity. I like looking at men when they get a hard-on and their eyes take on a kind of misty, silky gleam. It's like, he's looking at you, but he doesn't see you. He's quite different, I think, when a man is looking at me like that, in those silky, misty moments, he's mine. And when afterwards, some ten minutes later, he snores or farts or washes his cock in the bathroom, then he's someone else's. Or he belongs to himself. Then I'm not interested anymore. Get it? I simply wanted Miki's eyes to go silky, misty brown. For him to stop being a lawyer and become an animal between my legs. Not a beast. Beasts get on my nerves. You know, tearing underwear, hurling panties and boxer shorts into the air, breaking the hooks on your bra. A good bra costs a lot of money. And no one is so crazed with passion that he can't calmly undo a bra. Except in films. But films aren't life. And they're made by men. Screwing in films, that's just food for jerking off. I've got a friend. He's really crazy. He likes porno films. He travels around the world buying porno films, and brings them home. And his wife would rather die than say 'cunt' or 'cock.' Not a chance. Crazy woman. A virgin with two grown-up children. And he collects those films. And he told me what it's like at the Frankfurt airport. There are some booths there. You go in, sit down in front of the screen, quite close, so it seems you've got your nose right in a big cunt. Or something like that. That's how my friend, at that airport before his flight, sits with his nose in a big cunt. Men are insane. What woman would think of moaning in an armchair in a booth at an airport while waiting for a plane? Every normal woman is afraid of flying and certainly the last thing to occur to her, before getting on the plane, is to watch a big prick on a big screen and prepare herself for her flight like that. My friend swore to me that he doesn't jerk off in the booth. He just looks at the film. He swore by his two then-small children. I believe him. Not because he swore. I get fed up with people who keep saying 'on my children's lives,' as though 'children' were something inherently sacred, so if you swear on their lives, that's that. And all of us who have children know how sacred they are to us. Children are a pain in the ass. A worry. And nothing but a worry. A child is a beast that sucks you and sucks you, until it sucks you dry. Until you turn into a shell without that soft bit in the middle. And now you swear on the life of something that sucks you dry and turns you into something that is no longer you but only your frame, an empty house where you no longer live, because you don't live, not only in that house, but anywhere, and now swear on that and on top of it all expect someone to believe you. Pure crap. Swearing on our greatest enemies as though

-58-

they were the most important thing we have! Bullshit! We all hate our children. Our children have fucked us up. Disappointed us. Betrayed us. Our children are everything we once were ourselves. Cowardly or mindlessly obnoxious. Silent shits in a corner or brave morons fighting for human rights. It's all the same thing. You and me and them are all the same. Terrified assholes trembling before the bill collectors or fighters for union rights holding a piece of cardboard on Ban Jelačić Square. Demanding justice. Waiting for justice. They are our children. Eternally waiting. Exactly the same as us, only younger. It's crap living in hard times, so they can't pay for their sins themselves. So we pay for them. With our pensions, our apartments, our frayed nerves . . . I'll take a tranquillizer. Three 5mg ones. I swallow them. Without water. Kiki doesn't know that I have six boxes of them. If he did there'd be trouble.

Once I took a whole bottle. I wanted to kill myself. Yes. That was a real mess. You never wanted to kill yourself? What a lying shit you are! Why did you want to kill yourself? What was the big problem? What brought about the great explosion in your head? 'Big.' 'Big.' 'Big.' You're obsessed with big outcomes and big problems. Why shouldn't a person kill himself because of a little problem? Or without any problem at all? For the sake of his soul? That's never crossed your mind?

Great. You think that you have a mind. That's great. Maybe every attempted suicide has to be explained. Rummage through your grey matter. Find a reason. A difficult childhood. Your mother's a whore. Your father fucked you on your sixth birthday. Your father's called Živko, and you live in Croatia. War. Poverty. You can't afford a dentist or electricity. Your child has leukemia and you can't afford the cytostatic! You have to find a reason! There's always a reason for a person to want to kill himself. And do you know what's been troubling me my whole life? Finding one single fucking reason to live. Why in the hell do you want to live? Look at me. I was born in Opatija. My mother didn't want to take the Jewish apartment. She didn't want any kind of apartment, so we spent our lives in a cellar. I spent all my high-school years in other people's dresses without a top left incisor. I didn't laugh because of that top left incisor that I didn't have. I went to teacher-training college. Only retarded and poor people studied there. For three years I walked down the Corso in the same black skirt that I put water on to make it less shiny. I met Kiki while I was at the lousy college, and we got married, and . . . And so on. And my Kiki is a loser. No money, apart from when he sells some stolen clothing. And Aki is dragging herself through the university like a cat with a broken leg because we can't pay five hundred marks for each exam. This is what I'm telling you about. Someone ought to ask both you and me why we don't kill ourselves. At least I've tried. While you, morons, haven't even got the balls to do that. I swallowed a mountain of those pills and fell asleep. Then I woke up in the hospital. Kiki was crying beside my bed. Sobbing. I found that strange. Why is Kiki crying? Why doesn't he understand me when we're in the same film? If he doesn't understand me, who will? Get it? And he asked me:

'Why, why, why . . . ?'

That's when I realized, for the first time, that Kiki and I are in two different worlds. That our film isn't 'ours' but mine. Kiki's in some other film. Get it? Because, if that wasn't the case, why would he be asking me why, why, why . . . How could he ask me such a thing? I find it odd, I find it crazy that all Croats, all citizens of the Republic of Croatia, don't kill themselves. What in hell are they waiting for? Why are they waiting? Why don't you kill yourselves? Isn't it crazy, crazy, crazy to live only so that God grants us a peaceful death? Isn't that crap? Yes! Only you don't think about it. You're just damn stupid and that's why you don't kill yourselves. What nice things happen to you? What nice things are going to happen? New elections? Is that what you're waiting for! Ha, ha, ha, ha . . . I would die laughing if I ever laughed. But I never laugh, because of that top left tooth that I have but forget that I do.

I'm a bit tired, but I don't feel sleepy. I want to be awake to hear the doorbell ring. Yes. I'm lying here made up, foundation, lipstick, mascara, I'll just jump out of my pyjamas into jeans. And grab Miki by the balls. I thought of doing it with my left hand, but my left arm is more and more sore. Because of that accident this morning. I was sorry when they woke me up in the hospital. That's probably how everyone feels who's swallowed pills or some other shit. You want to change something in your life, but they pump out your stomach. And talk to you. I had a young woman doctor talk to me. Big blue eyes, thin, white coat. Tall.

'I understand you. Life is hard these days. Not only for you, for everyone. But why don't you think of your loved ones who love you so much?'

Really! Why should my fucking languishing (great word 'languishing') in this world be an aphrodisiac for my loved ones? Who am I living for? Who does my life belong to? My life! My life! What's mine if my life isn't mine? Do I have any rights at all? If I don't have the right to die, what do I have the right to? To my own life to make my nearest and dearest happy? And what if I don't give a shit about my nearest and dearest? What if I want to please myself? And fall asleep?

Fucking insomnia's killing me! Killing me! I don't know about you, but I'm sick to death of insomnia. I could spend my entire life awake. And I do. These old people on the screen just keep on wailing. 'Wailing,' a combination of crying, quiet crying and loud, penetrating noises, but not screams . . . They just keep on wailing.

'When did you first think of . . . this . . . ?' asked the doctor.

'When did I first think of killing myself?' I clarified.

'Yes,' said the doctor.

'On my twelfth birthday,' I said.

'Why?' asked the doctor.

There, you see? What a stupid, stupid, stupid question! Why? What was the cause? What happened to me? Was the cake too small? Had my mom smacked me? How can I explain to this sweet-smelling cow with the light-pink polish on her nails why I wanted to kill myself on my twelfth birthday? We were in the garden. In front of the cellar in which my mother, my grandmother and I lived. I had got a beautiful dress from Grandmother—green, and a tulle petticoat, pink. My Auntie Žora had made a cake because my mother doesn't know how to make cakes. Nor does

Gran. I blew out the candles, my little friends and I drank coke and then it occurred to me that none of this made any sense whatsoever. I went into our bedroom, my mother and I slept together, sat down on the double bed and looked into the mirror of my psyche—the psyche is a little chest of drawers with a mirror on it. It's called a psyche because it has a mirror and a person looks in the mirror for their soul, their psyche. I sat on that bed and looked into the mirror at my collar bone. When I was a child, being thin wasn't fashionable, nor were collar bones. What was fashionable were hidden collar bones under flesh and little girls who could wear skirts even without petticoats. My skirt just hung even with a petticoat. Nothing could keep my petticoat wide on my thin hips. I looked at my collar bones which were not covered in fat like my best friend Keti's. And then, as I was looking in the mirror, it occurred to me that one should kill oneself. That there was no sense whatever in screwing yourself your whole life and then in the end dying in terrible torment. I probably already guessed that I wouldn't have the money for an injection with some kind of drug. I'd die without anything. None of that is the point. I want to say something else. Why didn't I kill myself then? How did I find some sense in life? I simply told myself, if Keti doesn't ask herself this kind of question, and I knew that my best friend didn't ask herself anything, then I won't either. If Keti lives, I shall too. So many Ketis in the world don't talk with themselves, so I'll stop looking at my collar bones as well. But that was when I was twelve. And a person gets older. You're not the same at twelve and . . . I'm not going to tell you how old I am. When it's a question of my age, I'm a head without a tongue. I really like that expression. *Really* like it. 'A head without a tongue.' Great! That young doctor in her white, unbuttoned coat took me to the oncology department. Let me see how people fight for their lives with their hands and feet and heads without a single hair on them. And for chemotherapy that they can't afford and radiation they have to wait months for. Let me see that they don't ask themselves stupid questions and don't look at their collar bones. Although they are bald and rotten and yellow and poor and have had mastectomies and little colostomy bags and no intestines or bladders, they're all full of joy. Joy? Get it? A person has to get cancer in order to enjoy life to the full! While I, thank God, alive and healthy and surrounded by the care of my nearest and dearest, I want everyone to go to hell and I selfishly swallow pills. Who gives me the right to such callousness? And arrogance? Is there, after all, anywhere in me even the slightest trace of remorse? What a good, good word! 'Remorse.' No. But I didn't say that to the stupid doctor. And I wanted to say all sorts of things. I wanted to. She's young. At the beginning of her lousy life's journey. I wanted to say: Listen, you're going to spend your life with people like me. And with colleagues with whom you will compete tooth and nail for every conference you want to go to. You'll go looking around for workmen to paint your department. You'll say you've found 'sponsors.' When the workmen paint your department, your boss will send you to another department. Unpainted. You'll pay for every conference with your cunt or cash that you'll milk from some Kiki who will cry beside some Tonka. You'll have a baby. The child will be stupid like its father and unambitious. Maybe it'll stick a needle into its vein at thirteen. At seventeen for sure. Your husband, a doctor, will work nights three times a week and on weekends and screw the nurses. Everyone will know. Including you. Doctor, I would give a lot of money, a whole lot of money to be by your bed when you wake up, if they manage to wake you (doctors are more skillful than us amateurs) and say: 'My dear, dear lady, why did you do this to your loved ones?' Bitch, bitch who understands nothing. Nothing.

Ask the good Lord where you are. Are you here? You're here. I have to tell you this. While we're on the subject of where you are, here you are. I had a nephew. OK. I still have one. But he's not little anymore. And this happened when he was three or four. We were playing hide-and-seek at my sister's. My brother-in-law had hidden the kid, and I had to find him. I was young then. 'Full of life,' someone who didn't know me would have said. My brother-in-law's a moron. Really. A real moron. Not a special one. The most ordinary moron. And he hid little Biki. For him hiding a four-year-old kid in an apartment more than thirty square meters in size was war. A matter of life and death. He wanted to prove to me at any price that I couldn't find Biki. That I was too stupid. He would hide him in the dirty laundry basket. I didn't look for the kid at all. I would just shout: 'Where's Biki?' And Biki would call cheerfully from the basket: 'Here's Biki!' My brother-in-law would beat him. With a belt. He thought I would take pity on the beaten child. After the sixth or seventh hiding-place, he could hardly walk. And I would call: 'Where's Biki?' He would whisper: 'Here's Biki!' What was my brother-in-law trying to prove? What did I want to prove to him? People are strange. On the whole they don't understand each other at all. And you think you know me because we are spending the night together. We've already spent part of it. The major part of it. I'll tell you everything. I'm a tongue without a head. Miki will soon be ringing our doorbell.

Now where was I? Yes. Then I undid my dress. Yves Saint Laurent. The dress was out of this world. Miki watched me. Women are usually unsure of themselves. There aren't many women who have the guts to undress in front of a complete stranger and be the first to start the game. Except in films. But film scripts are written by men. We women never undress in front of strange men, we don't look them in the eye, we don't say: 'Fuck me.' But I said 'Fuck me' to Miki. Not because I'm brave or because I'm very old and don't care. No. I didn't give a shit whether he was going to fuck me or not. Get it? I didn't care. He could have said: 'Madam,' and then anything, the way men refuse women. I don't know anything about that, since no man has ever refused me. Lucky? Beautiful? No man has ever refused me because men have never particularly interested me. Or women. Kiki had simply brought me to this apartment a hundred years ago. And we've been together ever since. Men have approached me. Lots of them. Men go for married women. Married women radiate. They send out the message: 'I don't need a man.' That turns them on.

They've groped me. At Eighth of March celebrations at the firm, at sporting events, on business trips, at my desk in my office, on all Jadroplov ships, where I was a correspondent. But men didn't interest me. They left me cold. No. I'm not frigid. I'm not saying I never got aroused in my life. That I never came. That I don't know what an orgasm is. You just don't get it. Men simply didn't interest me. They're predictable. I won't say dull, stupid, boring, because that wouldn't be fair. I haven't met all the men who roam the world. I'm only talking about the men I've met. What I mean is, I've not been lucky. But, when someone says 'I've not been lucky,' it sounds as though you regretted something. Like, I regret the fact that I've never met the owner of a cock that would knock me off my feet. 'Knock me off my feet.' Powerful expression. Let me be completely clear. I haven't been lucky, but then again, I don't give a shit. I have never experienced the relationship between a man and a woman as a drama. All those murders and suicides for love and jealousy and that fear that the man you love will leave you, all of that is just plain crap to me. He'll leave me? Let him! Who gives a fuck! What'll I lose if Kiki leaves me? OK, Kiki isn't going to leave me, I'm going to leave him, or that well-known expression 'let's say,' so let's say Kiki leaves me. What in hell's name will happen to me? Nothing. Apart from the fact that I'll be left without a prick that I don't need. And don't want, that oppresses me. And which I know from its root to its tip, and back to its root and the hairs on his ass. I'll have no status? I won't be a Married Woman but an Abandoned Woman. In relation to whom? To you? You who are listening to me? I've already told you that I don't give a shit what you think of me. So, men don't interest me. But their desire sometimes amuses me.

I don't know when men stopped looking at me. I couldn't say when that happened. On which day, in which year. You don't notice it. When I was young, we wore mini-skirts up to our pussies. We walked through the world dressed in almost nothing but a short skirt. I used to think then that I'd never become like one of those old women who looked at me full of hate. I was certain that old age happened only to other people. That my legs would always be long, firm and thin. My tits big and high. My eyes clear even at five in the morning after a sleepless night. At that time I thought that everyone fell asleep as soon as their heads hit the pillow. Once on the beach in Opatija, an old woman got sick. The ambulance came, and there, in front of everyone, they undressed her and did something with her mouth. Perhaps they were taking out her false teeth. That was the first time in my life I saw an old pussy. Almost hairless. Just a few grey ones flattened on a dried-up mound. Poor woman, I thought. It seemed to me that old age was a kind of illness, that an old dried-up pussy wouldn't happen to me, but to you. And yours. That's what I think now as well. When I look in the mirror, I think that what I see will be passable. That the two light brown patches under my eyes are from sunbathing although I don't sunbathe, that my ass is a big fat orange only because of chocolate. But I don't worry too much. I regret I'm old for purely aesthetic reasons. I'd prefer in the morning, in the mirror, to see a face like Aki's. But on the other hand, I don't want to be young the way the young are young. I wouldn't want to be twenty now and have to pay for every exam with sex. Being young didn't used to be in fashion the way it is today. Cunts weren't stars, they didn't give interviews, they didn't say what they thought about the war, peace, tourism, the jagged Croatian coast line, mine-clearing and the beauties of Dubrovnik. Cunts were cunts. In offices, schools, universities, in official cars, hotels, between bosses' knees. There weren't so many of them. In my time few girls used their cunts to make their way through the world. It's different now. And that confuses me. OK. I don't give a shit. I'm not competing. Even if I wanted to I wouldn't be able to buy anything with my cunt. Miki, who's going to ring the bell at seven tomorrow morning or this morning, won't be ringing it because of my cunt. He loves me. I'm talking about cunts, not me. Today Croatia is run by cunts. In the papers, on television, on the radio . . . A fifteen-year-old creature with big tits and long legs gives interviews all over the place about what she thinks about Bin Laden. She'll sail off to the Seychelles and become the most beautiful woman in the world. And tell the truth about Croatia. Another will go to the Caribbean. There she'll use her cunt to draw attention to Croatian mine fields. A third goes to America to use her cunt to tell Bush that she's worried about the fierce unrest in the Middle East. Cunts, cunts, cunts, cunts . . . Everything in Croatia revolves around young cunts. They are the headlines, the main topics, the top story and breaking news. I'm not jealous. Nor do I think it would be good, if instead of young cunts in the Seychelles talking about the beauties of Croatia, that fat pricks between young legs were to do it. That's not what I mean. OK. You don't like these expressions. They're too strong. Cock. Cunt. Fucking. Prick. And out of the mouth of a woman. And an older woman! I see that. I accept it. I confess. OK. And I don't give a fuck. You are all cunts. You let yourselves be manipulated. You let people feed you the hottest topic, the success of some cunt in a far-off warm sea, instead of saving your ass from hunger. But, when someone tells you that, when they point it out with the best possible intentions, when they open your stupid, dull, blind eyes, then that person's the one with a problem! I've got a problem? Me? I say cunt, cock, fuck? And you're not adults? If you were little, you'd be asleep now. But even little kids and the smallest ones in pre-school know what a cunt and a cock are. Only they don't make a fuss about it. As long as they're very small. Until they understand. As soon as they begin to grasp something, the grown-ups start explaining what a cock and a cunt are, and that fucking is something wrong. 'Don't take any notice,' they say to their visitors. 'Don't laugh and they'll give up.' No one has ever written up to what age mentioning a cunt and a cock provokes only laughter. Three, six, five? You don't get it at all, do you? Not a single thing! As soon as you, as a little, snotty kid, agreed to say cock only under your breath and only when grown-ups couldn't hear you, you capitulated to the manipulation. Cock and cunt are only the beginning. That's how power trains you by imposing discipline. Other things come later. Study, wash your hands, go to church, play the violin, learn solfeggio, play soccer, study, get a degree, don't masturbate, play the lottery, and show off your ass in the Caribbean. Get it! Here!

Here! Here! Come on! Cunt! And they don't give a fuck what you think about it. Whether all those solfeggios and all that parading your shaved cunt really interest you. Maybe what you'd like, maybe what all of you want is to spend your lives stroking a rabbit's warm back. Or selling tea on a Vienna square. They have great tea there. And there's a Greek joint as well where an American woman from Florida serves breakfast at lunchtime. And you can even buy shoes from American army surplus stores. Secondhand. But new as well. There's no difference in price. OK. I get it. My nocturnal lecture is getting on your nerves. But what will you do with yourselves, if you stop listening to me? How will you spend the night? What the hell will you do till morning? What'll you do in the morning? What do you actually do? Eh, Croats!!! OK. You're not all Croats. OK. I didn't mean Croats. I meant citizens of the Republic of Croatia. And what if people across the border are listening to me? Why don't I say something in Slovene as well? Maybe Slovenes are listening to me too? OK. Great! I like it when you're caustic and in such a wonderful mood. I don't know Slovene. And I don't give a shit about the Slovenes. But wait. Has it occurred to you that you feel good because you're with me? Is my good mood infectious? And now your depression isn't so bad. I'm surprised, no kidding, that you manage to get through your lives. Without panic? Screaming? Fury? That you don't want to get out of your cages that you've paid for a hundred times? Why don't you organize yourselves into duos, trios, or quartets? Why don't you drag shells and grenade launchers out of your cupboards and cellars? And kill these bastards who screw you on TV? OK. Not now! Not this moment! That Tearful Sack is still showing the refugees her shaved legs. Fuck your tears, you cow! That would be criminal? What I'm encouraging you to do? What would it be? Inciting a rebellion? Destroying the constitutional order? Revolution? Spreading hatred? And you'll report me to the authorities, you shits. You forget that it's night, that all of this is just a conversation, that no one can hear us. That *they* can't hear us. *They* hear everything. Ha! So you're paranoid too? They told me, when I was in the hospital, that paranoia is an illness. That *they* don't exist. That it's an illusion. That's typical of this illness. And that *they'll* go away, if I do as I'm told, if I'm good and take the medicine. So, ladies and gentlemen, either you're ill, and *they* don't exist, or *they* exist. Do you follow? You do. OK. I accept that. If *they* don't exist, except in demented heads like mine (this is you talking now) who should you kill, who should you eliminate, who should you stick the grenade launcher into the mouth of, if you can do that with a grenade launcher at all? Yes. That's the right question. OK. One for you. Two for you, ten for you and nothing for me! OK! I yell this. To make sure you hear me. You're that anxious to beat me? To prove that you're right? Why? I don't give a fuck about you. This is just a conversation. I'm not the least bit tense. I'm just saying what I think. This is a free, democratic country. I'm not reacting. My hands aren't shaking. And my palms aren't sweating. But, you are in trouble. You think your pathetic lives have some meaning. Come on. I'm listening to you now. I'm not saying you ought to shoot a bullet into your mouth where half your teeth are missing! I'm not persuading you to do anything. Don't bullshit! I'm not giving you my recipe for doing things. Like I'm some kind of example. I failed. Something woke me up. I'm listening. I'm listening. Do you hear? I'm listening! When was the last time someone listened to you? Really listened? Didn't wait for you to shut your mouth so that he could open his. Have you ever watched your children when you're talking to them? When I'm telling my Aki something, she watches me, and with her right hand fiddles with her cell phone, sending text messages. 'Go on, I'm listening!' Then I talk. I don't want her thinking I know that she's not listening. Get it? I don't want her to feel awkward. I behave as though Aki were someone who loves me. Like hell she does. She doesn't give a fuck about me. She has her life about which I know nothing. Because I never listen when she talks to me. And she does talk to me. She likes talking to me. But she doesn't like it when I reply. Because, I don't reply, I talk. Each of us has her own story. When I was little, we had music at school. I never had any talent for music. Miki likes music. Not Kiki, Miki! All right, Kiki likes music too! But Miki has a real feeling for it. I don't even know how to put on a CD. Or a video. Or send a fax. Or turn on a computer. Or how to surf the net. Or chat. Or send an email. And we do have a computer and a laptop. We've got everything. All stolen. A cell phone too. I don't have a cell phone. And I never will! I hate noises. Of any kind. I hate music. All kinds. And the sound of telephones. And cell phones. And the buzzing of fat, fleshy, black flies. Then I turn the light out in the bedroom, and put it on in the hallway, and when the fleshy piece of shit goes towards the light, I shut the bedroom door, put on the light, and listen to the repulsive creature banging against the glass door. In vain. I like silence. Silence. Without CDs, flies, cell phones, human voices, children's cheerful squeals, tin instruments, drum majorettes, carnival parades. Silence. Silence. Yes. I didn't like that music lesson. So in the fourth year of elementary school I got a mark of one out of ten for conducting. I spent some time explaining to my mother how difficult conducting was. Single-time, triple-time, quadruple-time, beat, I mean. You wave, always differently and who knows why? I explained to my mother that conducting was really hard and I simply couldn't get it. She didn't listen to me. She kept repeating: 'An F in music? What's wrong with you? There's something wrong with you! There must be something wrong with you.' It was then that I took an oath. You don't believe me? I told you that we lived in a basement. Out of the kitchen window I watched human feet going up and down the steps. I watched people like that cartoon cat watches the legs of a fat black woman. You never see anything of that black woman except her fat legs. That's how I saw nothing except legs either. Fat. Thin. Men's. Women's. Children's. Covered up in winter. Bare in summer. People always dropped things in front of the basement window, which was our kitchen. As though that window wasn't the window of our kitchen. But a basement where there were nothing but rats and wood. But that wasn't a problem. The men kept spitting in front of the window. Expectorating, actually. (Great word!) That noise really got to me, I don't like noises in any case, but if you were to ask me, if you were to ask me which is the most loathsome noise, I wouldn't say air-raid sirens. Although I heard them during the war. And it was terrible. Because the siren would howl when I was sitting on the heater, reading something, and Aki was at school. And that was terrible. That feeling that the city was going to be shelled and Aki and I would die a long way from one another. She in her school, I on this heater. I didn't know, I couldn't have known that every siren may mean shells, but it needn't. It was my first war. OK. That was terrible. But still. What I'm telling you about was worse. When those men would stop in front of our window, dredge up phlegm, snorting, really trying to drag as much as possible out of their sinuses or some other hole in their heads, and then chuck it all out in front of our window. My mother kept washing with hot water and sweeping with a broom whatever those men left for us. All right. I'll describe our kitchen. I was sitting in a corner, and my mother beside the wood stove. It was lit. OK. I could say that the fire was burning brightly, but it wasn't. If it had been, I would have told you. My mother looked at me, I looked at her. Then I told her about that bad grade in music. And then she said what I told you. There, you see it's true. Then I swore an oath that I would listen to my children. Really listen. That I would be interested in what those children were saying to me. I wouldn't be somewhere else. I wouldn't just look at them. My children and I would be in the same film. There, you see. What does swearing an oath mean? What does 'I swear' mean? Nothing. Not a damn thing. I don't listen to Aki. Ever. And I never did. My happiest days with Aki were when she was sick in bed, with a temperature, and I watched Italian television. *Pronto, Raffaella*! At that time I thought that people could have several lives. My life with little Aki and Kiki—who was the officer in charge of General National Defense and Social Self-Defense, and got the sack and now deals in ties and suits, you know that—that this life with little Aki and Kiki was something temporary. That it would pass. Like a pimple in the hairs of your eyebrow. And then I'd start over and be *Pronto, Tonka*! And look at the camera and smile and say: 'Pronto, pronto' . . . I liked taking Aki to a sand pile, there was a building site near this building, she would spend hours rolling in the sand, and I'd be in another life. A life without Aki, without Kiki, without debts, without going to the office where all the women except for me crocheted and knitted. That's a terrible feeling. That really depressed me. If she didn't take her mid-morning break, my co-worker Koka would make a white mohair scarf in eight hours. The whole scarf would be a large spider's web, snow white, with big, soft spiders tangled in it. It was a real work of art. Of course I don't like spiders. I've got a broom so I give them hell, when I have the time. That's not what I'm talking about. Some people say it's bad luck to kill spiders. You should throw them gently out of the window. OK. You do what you like. I don't always slaughter them myself. When I'm in trouble, when I'm upset, then I pick them up by a leg and throw them. When I'm not upset, when I'm sure of myself, then . . . then I slaughter them. Something has just occurred to me. I told you that I pick the spider up by the leg . . . At Jadroplov there were lots of women. There were lots of mice as well. In that old building. Then Živko, yes, his name was Živko, the secretary of our section . . . Huh, it's only just occurred to me that he might have been a Serb. But maybe not. That Catholic priest who's forever bullshitting in the newspapers, he's called Živko too, presumably he's not a Serb. No matter. Živko spread paper plates with glue, put little pieces of cheese and pancetta on them, and the mice got caught. Their shrieks ripped through our brains. Once he caught three little mice, and then their old mother or father mouse rushed to the rescue, then the mother was joined by the father, or the father by the mother, and the whole family was caught. OK. That's not why I'm telling you this. We had a dentist and a doctor and someone who made coffee who were all working there at that time. And cheap coffee. And that woman who made coffee came into her little kitchen in the morning and saw three little mice glued to the plate. And the two big mice. The parents. OK. You don't have to believe me. I don't swear I'm telling the truth and nothing but the truth. I don't have a Bible at my bedside table, so I've nothing to swear by. Besides, you know what I think about oaths and curses. This is true. She cut those mice's feet off so 'they wouldn't suffer.' 'So they could go where they wanted.' She liberated them. What does that remind you of? Nothing? And now tell me, prove to me that people are not stupid! Stupid pricks! I was tormented by the fact that I didn't know how to crochet. That I didn't fit in. That I wasn't good at anything. Tanja was capable of crotcheting three pairs of slippers during the five hours of our working day. And then Goca got a job with us. I meet her now on the Corso from time to time. She was sacked. She took me under her wing at that time. And with great love, and patience, patience, patience, she demonstrated that everything was possible when you really wanted it. And so for one Easter, with my own hands, yes, my own fingers, I crocheted six egg holders out of bright yellow mohair wool. In the shape of chicks. On each chick I made a black eye, out of ordinary wool, and a red beak out of mohair. And then I put the little chicks on six large eggs. I felt good! Good! Really good! Like after an orgasm. Immediately after an orgasm. Not five minutes later. Because by then the messages are already reaching your brain, that you have to move your ass, get the chicken out of the freezer, iron a shirt for tomorrow, do the dishes because you fucked after lunch, and take all the socks out of the basket and try to find at least six that make up three pairs. Why am I telling you about the yellow chicks? Yes. Those chicks moved me. Reminded me of happy memories. So I'm not angry anymore. So I don't want to tell you what crap your life is. You're right! Who am I to take a shit on your life? Maybe you're happy! Maybe you don't give a damn about details. Maybe you're easygoing and not at all angry. People are different. And you don't have to look at the world through my eyes. I'm aggressive. I like fucking with your head. I'm the same as the people I'm telling you about. The people who perhaps exist, or perhaps they don't. Perhaps they don't exist. Perhaps we are the only people who do? Perhaps everyone is the architect of their own fate? That's what we learned in high school. Perhaps this talk of 'them' who screw us up is just an alibi for us cowards who don't have the balls to take life into our own hands? 'We'? 'Us'? Why am I 'we' all of a sudden? You're right. OK. You see how good I am. I always feel good when I confess some fault. Or mistake. When I see that someone else is right. Fighting makes me tired. Gets on my nerves. 'I'm tired, my friend, tired . . .' That's the song my Kiki listens to when he's alone and when he thinks no one can hear it. When he thinks I can't hear him. Other people like that song. Other people? Our friends. They are the 'other people.' Yes. We have friends. But I'm not going to list their names now. They wouldn't mean anything to you. They really can't figure me out. They just don't get it. They think that people are essentially good. That all the killings and slaughter around us, this war in the Balkans and this fighting over the Taliban or fighting in some other hellhole, they think those things are just a nuisance that can be figured out. That war breaks out when there's a problem to be solved. That war is always something temporary, until the trouble's fixed. And it's a nuisance when the Serbs attack us, and want to kill us. And all we want is to defend ourselves. And leave everyone where he belongs. And when we kill Serbs in Croatian towns, when we drag them out of their apartments into the cellar or into a field and put a bullet in the back of their heads, that's a war of self-defense too. And when we tie their hands behind their backs with wire and shove them into the river running under our bridge, that's self-defense as well. Or when we drive all of them out of their houses and set them on fire, that's just a response to what they did to us. Because they started it. And if 'they' start it, then everything else is a response of the 'just' who are where they belong. You are only defending what's yours. I won't say 'we' are defending what's ours because I shouldn't barge my way in among you because of damn Živko. You can't sit by with your arms folded while a Chetnik screws your mother. I can see that. We can agree about that. Some of that. That's what all my friends think. I understand. I can grasp the fact that some workman in the middle of Zagreb can kill a little girl and throw her into a pit because she's a Serb. I can understand that you don't give a shit about that because you're Croats and because there was a war on and that's the way things were. Everyone has a right to his opinion. Besides, in the wild Balkans there never was peace. And never will be. Today it was their little girl, tomorrow someone will shove a knife or a prick into my Aki in the middle of town. I see that. I understand. But I still can't stand it when these guys from Europe come and start giving me shit about how all of this around us is happening just because I'm Zivko's daughter. I don't like that. I don't appreciate that. I don't believe it. That my Živko was an animal. The only one on the planet. I think that we are all Živkos. War, violence, slaughter, rape, throat-slitting, eye-gouging and fucking other people's mothers in the ass. That is normal human behavior. Wiping one's nose with Kleenex, not smoking on buses, not spitting on the floor, not shoving a knife into your neighbor's throat is what's imposed on you. Dictatorship. Whose? Theirs? Who are they? You're not listening to me. *They* are our masters. *They* are the ones who say: 'Kill!' or 'Wipe your nose!' I suspect that we are all cutthroats, Aki, Kiki, Miki and my mother and me. Just give us a chance. Each of us has somewhere an eye which we'd gouge out of someone's face, or the back of a head where we'd put a bullet or an ass we'd shove our prick into out of hatred. War is something where every normal person feels at home. Normal person! Each where they belong. Everyone, fuck it. The fucking Americans and Norwegians and Italians and Germans and my shitty Živko. We all feel a warm glow as we slit other people's daughters' throats. We feel good, feel relieved. Human at last. But. And this is the only catch. War has its 'sell-by' date. One day the masters decide. It's time to pick up the buckets in the sand box, take the spades out of the sand. That's always the trouble. Because we've just got going. This is when it's best, when we've set fire to the sixth house and dragged out the ninth fridge, fucked the child on the doorstep . . . Over. Over? Over?! How can it be over? What 'rules of the game'? Someone says that children playing in the sand box are throwing the sand too far and too high. Some buckets are missing. Suddenly it's not normal to fuck their little girls. There. That's what I don't like. That's hypocritical. People are always raping someone's little daughter or fucking someone's mother in the ass. I saw it, people felt comfortable in the war. The great majority of people. All normal people felt good in the war. Good. Good and righteous. Most did. You can scream, sing patriotic songs, wave pretty flags, put one on the roof, a big one, let it flutter, you can slaughter, you can steal, you can kill half a town in the name of justice and truth. And it would be great if the war could last forever. But it doesn't last. That's what's giving us grief. You and me. They decided there shouldn't be any more war. You think that war is waged by a president and peace is agreed to by two presidents. You've got to be joking. Presidents only sign things. They don't decide. Clinton didn't even decide which hooker would suck his cock. They were brought to him according to his masters' criteria. Presidents? Presidents are bears at a circus. Who's the Gypsy at the other end of the chain? Who gives orders to Clinton and our masters? The same ones who ordered us to play in the sand and gave us buckets and shovels, are now driving us away. Over. Closing time. Time out. And *they're* still fucking us. They say that so much slaughter wasn't normal. How much slaughter *is* normal? They don't say. They talk bullshit. They blame us. They impose peace. And we'd go on playing. Till death. But no. Now we must answer their questions. Who fucked the old woman without a left leg? Whose wife had nine cocks in her in just one night? Whose cocks were they? Ours? Theirs? Is nine too many? Or too few? Or is that the right number? Little girls had to give blow-jobs to drunken soldiers. How many soldiers were there? Why were they drunk? Who was in charge? Who was their commander? And in fact who cares? Who gives a shit about fucked little girls and slit throats? Can the little girls walk as though they had not had a hundred pricks between their legs? No. So? What court can heal so many little cunts? None. *They're* playing with us. Our masters are screwing all of us. First they let us be what we are: rapists, cutthroats, fuckers, gravediggers, arsonists, suffocators, peeeooople . . . People! And then overnight we must wipe our noses with handkerchiefs. No one's going to put anything over on me! I know that there are those who begin and end the game. They need a break. A rest. To divide the spoils. To fuck young loudmouths without a lot of commotion, cut ribbons in the color of the Croatian flag or the color of some other flag, and look at the bare legs of the cunt offering them the scissors. Without smoke or tanks or shells or knives. So they can take little boys off on yachts and screw them on the deck. Or take them to hunt tigers. And then in the cool tent stick their pricks into their narrow little asses. They can be photographed with the wife they haven't fucked for nine years, but that doesn't bother the wife because she's being fucked by a twenty-year-old kid for just a thousand marks a month. What have we all done, you and I and my Kiki and Miki and everyone I know so that this old shit who is right now looking at me from the TV screen can talk bullshit about what he's going to give up for Lent? You've burned down thousands of houses, killed a million people, screwed a thousand children so that this old shit can hold his old wife by the hand and talk bullshit about what he's going to buy her for Christmas? Get it? *They're* playing with us. This whole war was waged just so that this fat, rich, old shit could shove himself between my legs and my daughter's. For a hundred marks. All the wars on the planet are waged so that creeps can screw our daughters for a little money. I go nuts when I hear that we are the 'Balkans.' We are 'wild'! We are the only ones who slit throats, rape and burn. What about the Americans in Afghanistan? Those fuckers don't rape and burn?! When they shove their pricks into someone's ass, that's not screwing, that's spreading democracy? That's bullshit! The Americans bombed Belgrade . . . Hey, don't shout! Don't scream! The Americans were right! All right . . . OK. OK! They were right! I'm shouting this! Are you deaf, you motherfucker! I'm not saying the Americans weren't right! You fucking cunt! Now I'm going to speak slowly. The Americans bombed Belgrade. Come on, be quiet. They dropped some bombs, with some cold or enriched or depleted uranium that causes cancer. Let them get cancer! Let them get cancer! OK, let them, that's not what I'm talking about. Who gives a shit? I want to say something else. These same Americans who dropped bombs that cause cancer on Belgrade are now collecting money in Belgrade to help children with cancer. There are bald children in Belgrade, they sit them on their laps and have their photos taken with them, looking anxiously into the camera and asking for help! That's what I'm talking about! The way they're screwing them! The way they're screwing *you*! You and me! At least I know I've got a prick up my ass. Forever! And a day! But you just don't get it, fuck you. No, you feel guilty about everything you did in the war, as though war was something abnormal and crazy. So now, full of self-reproach, what a great word 'self-reproach,' with a fat prick up your ass, you cover your stupid head with ashes, rebuild the houses you burned down with such pleasure, and which maybe you wouldn't have burned down if you had known what fuckers you were doing it for. That! That! If you were smart—but you're not, you're a stupid imbecile with a prick up your ass—you would not be you. I get it, but I don't know what to do about it, I don't know how to use what I understand. If you and I were smart, you wouldn't be you and I wouldn't be me, we'd be them. The vile faces on the TV screen. And my Kiki would now be fucking some little piece of ass, and some little piece would be fucking me. Or not. But I would have the right to choose. Choose! Freedom is the right to choose. To screw! Or be screwed! To have the right to choose! You don't have it! And they took mine from me. When they woke me up in that goddamn room. That's what gets me.

And now I'll tell you how Miki and I first screwed. That means a lot in the relationship between a man and a woman. It doesn't mean anything in the relationship between a man and a woman. Women don't usually come because it's not easy to hold a strange cock in your hand, while men usually do come but they are tormented by doubt about whether they were any good because they think she came, she yelled, but they have a feeling that she didn't really. The uncertainty kills them. That's why she assures him that it was great. Really great. Finger-licking good, as my friend from the city of Split would say, I like him a lot, but he's not important here. Yes. I undid that dress, showed my tits in the black bra and silk slip and pantyhose. In a film Miki, crazed with passion, would have leapt at me, torn everything off me, thrown me across the armchair and fucked me. He would have moaned, I would have moaned and then together (fuck orgasm if it's not together) we would have come, yelling. But we weren't in a film, and Miki isn't crazy James Bond who can screw any time, any place. Miki is a lawyer who can't even pay (I didn't know that then) his membership to the lawyers' association. So, just a well-dressed guy without money. Films can screw up a person. Miki just looked at me. 'I don't understand,' he said when I said: 'Fuck me.' 'Fuck me,' I repeated. He looked at me. Not uninterested, no, but a bit confused. And he kept glancing towards the windows, although the blinds were almost completely closed. But I didn't feel like shit. I told you already. I didn't care. If he fucked me, good. If he refused me, that was good too. Miki didn't

-92-

refuse me. He just said: 'I don't understand.' And gave the ball back to me. So I was supposed to explain what the writer had meant to say. That was the most difficult thing. On the whole a writer doesn't mean to say anything. A writer writes, someone else explains. His main idea. The guiding thread. In that story I was the writer. And I was also supposed to be a 'teacher of the Croatian or Serbian language.' That's what it says on my diploma. After that Teacher's Training . . . Shit. So I looked at him, my dress open, in that stupid bra and slip and pantyhose. I felt like those poor bastards in the park when they open their coats and show a nun their big cock and she, instead of shrieking in horror and grabbing her rosary or something else hanging round her virginal neck, just stops, goes up to the big cock and takes it between her thumb and forefinger. That's how I felt. Like a pervert whose cock was being looked over by a nun. Horrible feeling. I sat down in the client's chair. Miki was sitting in the armchair that wasn't leather, he didn't know that yet. I hadn't collapsed onto the chair. I hadn't gone plop. I just sat down. And I didn't pull up my dress. I said:

'I don't really feel like fucking, but I like the curve of the back of your head and your thick lips and the curls on your neck.'

What balls. What a jerk.

'Relax,' said Miki. 'Take a deep breath. I don't think you're quite well. What happened?'

'Nothing,' I said, 'why should something have happened? Hasn't a woman ever said: "Fuck me" to you?'

'No,' said Miki, 'you're the first, and it's thrown me. What am I supposed to do? Leap on you?'

'Yes,' I said, but somewhat uncertainly.

Because his office was small and if he had leapt on me who knows what he would actually have leapt on. And there was a desk between us. He couldn't leap. He had to stand up, go round the desk, come up to me, lift me from the chair and take me somewhere where there was more space. So. Get it? That wasn't a place for wild passion. 'OK,' said Miki, 'let's go to the waiting room.' And now. Imagine a real imbecile. You think you know me, but you'd never guess what I said. I would never have guessed what I was going to say either. But I said: 'Do you like me at least a little bit?' What a cow! What an asshole! I open my dress, I say 'Fuck me' and then I interrogate and beg for a declaration of love. Like, it can't be pure fucking with no feeling, like, let it be love. And all the time, I don't give a shit about love, I know it isn't love, I don't even feel like fucking, I don't care about anything, but still

-94-

I want it to be something it isn't. As though someone were watching next to me, to the left or right, or above me. Someone I had to answer to. And say, you see, I'll do it, but I'm not a slut. As though it mattered whether I was a slut or not. As though anyone cared. As though a woman was a slut if she screwed a stranger in his office. A virtual stranger. And if she was a slut, what difference does that make? Get it? Constantly, always, ceaselessly, every moment in every day of my fucking life I answer unasked questions. I'm tired of it. I've had enough. There's a prejudice people have. Or I thought there was a prejudice, that intellectuals, men with degrees, lawyers, doctors, university teachers, solicitors, that they had small cocks. While dock workers and Serbs had big ones. You know, the size of the cock is in inverse proportion to the size of the brain. I had always thought and I think now, at this moment, that Miki is an intelligent man. Maybe that's what irritates me most. I like intelligent men. And women. Maybe because I'm stupid. That's why I like clever people. Mind you, it depends what my criteria are. OK. I'll be precise. So you don't get mad. I think that Miki is smart. That's bound to be a prejudice. I think he's smart because he's got a degree. I know a lot of people who have degrees and are dumb as shit. Forget that. It's not important. I expected that

Miki would have a small cock. And that would be a problem. That I'd have to console him. Assure him that size wasn't important, and I'd convince him, then probably have to guide him into me with my hand, until, with time, Miki gained some self-confidence. And self-assurance. Until the size, or rather lack of it, of his prick stopped being a problem. We women, I could swear to you, but I won't because you know how much I believe in oaths, we women are enormous idiots. Conceited bitches who think they know everything about men. And we know as much about them as they do about us. Nothing. So, when I caught sight of what was peering out of Miki's boxer shorts, I was shocked. You know. Completely speechless. A cartoon bubble above my head with a hundred-and-fifty question marks and a huge number of exclamations. Like some animal's penis with a huge, erect, round head was looking at me. OK. That's probably not true. I never measured it. That's how it seemed. The word 'salami' is an ugly word, filthy and inappropriate, but it really was a salami. Say the word 'salami' out loud and you'll get what I'm saying. A salami thirty centimeters long. Maybe a centimeter or two less. Not less than that. Between his legs Miki had a cock made for porno films and not for sitting on an uncomfortable wooden chair in a little courtroom, in which a neurotic woman judge, a typist, the future former husband, the future former wife and the lawyer of the future former husband hammer each other over a hundred kunas of alimony. I just stared. And then Miki completely undressed me, I had intended to undress him because at my age I could have been his much-older sister. He leaned me against the table in the waiting room and entered me. He moved in and out while I watched through the half-closed blinds what was going on in the boutique in the building across the street. The boutique is on the third floor. While Miki was screwing me I watched other women trying on coats. Long ones. Mura? God knows. I can't see too well without my glasses. They mostly looked at themselves. The young assistants dressed and undressed them. There was a dark red coat I liked, with red, rich, fake fur. It occurred to me that I could buy it when Miki was done with his orgasm, and I had washed in his restroom, and gotten dressed, and then walked down into the Corso and gone up to the boutique. I could buy that coat. But I already told you Kiki has a lot of good coats. All international labels. And it would really be too much for me to wear an unknown brand when you could have Aquascutum or Burburry. Although I always wear one black no-name brand coat bought on sale. You see, people are usually perverse. Yes. Miki came just as a tall, red-haired woman was paying by credit card for a green coat. Short. With no fur.

I haven't told you the details. Actually, I haven't told you anything. How he took off my pantyhose. Whether I helped him. Whether he took off his boxer shorts or simply pulled it out through the zipper ('zipper,' what a crazy word) nor how he took off my panties, how he put his hands on my ass, then turned me towards him, and we shuffled over to the couch, and I sat on the couch, and he knelt on the tiles of the waiting room, and . . . Yes. I haven't told you the details. And I won't. I wouldn't want you to start jerking off while I'm telling my story. Your heavy breathing would distract me.

And people are sick to death of fucking. Fucking and war stories. There, look at the screen, either they're fucking or there's an atomic bomb in the background or some other bomb lights them up as they jump into a trench. Those war stories make me sick. With their bombs, trenches, tanks, flares, blackened faces, planes, helihopters (that's how you say it, 'helihopters'), I'm sick to death of them. I like war documentaries. You know, from real life. But you very, very rarely come across one of them. There aren't any real war stories anymore. Aki and I really enjoyed the funeral of that baby. Come on, you remember . . . You must remember. That baby had been killed or had its throat slit or been thrown into cold water. Chetniks. Next-door neighbors. There's always a big to-do when your next-door neighbor turns on you. It makes it worse. A real jolt. You know, you have coffee together for thirty years, you take your children to school together on their first day, you watch soccer matches on television together, and then along comes the war and your neighbor murders your mother. Or throws your baby into the well. It's really serious. Aki and I watched the coverage of the funeral of that baby. It was great. We wept. It's a good feeling, really good, when you can have a good cry over someone else's misfortune. You've no idea how I sobbed when Lady Di died. I howled. I couldn't stop. And I used up a big box of Kleenex. We wept and sobbed. The baby's coffin was white and little and sweet. It was carried by four soldiers in camouflage. You know. Really dignified. They could hardly contain the tears in their eyes. They would have wept as well if they hadn't been heroes and soldiers, had they been ordinary people like any other ordinary people who are not under an obligation to their rank and uniform. They can howl, and sob and weep. The young mother had to be carried. She staggered after the coffin. Aki and I were crying our eyes out. They had to carry the young father along too. He was in a camouflage uniform. He had come straight from the battlefield to the funeral of his new-born baby. They carried the granny along too. She was probably the great-granny. Because the granny of such a little baby, the mother of such a young mother, could not have been older than me. Only younger. So, they carried the great-granny along too. The priest walked alone, without help, but evidently moved. Although funerals aren't hard for priests because they know that the dead go off to the sky and not to dust or ash and worms. But still the priest was sad. A person can always go off to the sky, there's plenty of time for that, he doesn't have to go as a baby, maybe that was what he was thinking, and that upset him. All the villagers in the procession had tears in their eyes. The women were sobbing, their husbands were supporting them. Some glanced out of the corner of their eye at the camera but the cameraman moved swiftly away. A TV journalist was covering the funeral live—as much as her tears and her light-pink made-up, trembling lips allowed. The corners of her mouth were dark, emphasized with a lip-line. On the screen we saw where the baby had had its throat cut or been thrown into the well. I re-member the garden and the well, but not the details. We saw photos of the baby's christening, water on its little head, the baby in a long white dress, everyone smiling round it, its plump little hands. The baby at its brother's birthday party. Third. Yes. The Chetniks had slit the brother's throat or thrown him into the well too, only six months earlier. Aki and I watched. And sobbed and wept and snivelled and wiped our noses and wept and sobbed and snivelled . . . Will you have your orgasm soon! You're a heartless pig! That's what you are! I didn't know then, while Aki and I were emptying our tear sacs, that the whole white funeral was a lie. We didn't have a clue. But it was a lie. Some old woman from TV made an announcement the other day and revealed the truth. The TV station had bought the little coffin and the flowers and the wreaths with white ribbons, they had paid the mother and the father and the old granny and the sad villagers and four soldiers. Yes, the priest too. The woman from TV said that what bothered her most was the way the four muscle-bound yokels in their splotchy clothes carried the little coffin. 'As though it was empty.' And the woman thought that was unconvincing. So that you or Aki or I who was watching the funeral might have guessed that it was all the most vile crap and a bare-faced lie. Like, the bearers ought to have been tottering from the effort. What a stupid bitch! As though it's a problem for Croatian heroes to carry seven kilos of dead weight! You know what? As far as I'm concerned, our television could have carried a live broadcast of the murder of tiny babies and cheerful little boys. That wouldn't have aroused murderous fury in me. I would not have rushed straight from the broadcast to the first line of the battlefield and sought an altar on which to lay down my life for the Homeland. It wouldn't have occurred to me. Or Kiki. We beat our brains out all through the war trying not to die, and not thinking how to give up our lives. I'm not saying that lots of kids died for nothing. I'm not saying that. Nor am I saying that they wanted to die for nothing. They died. It's a great blessing that they'll never know why. They didn't live to find out. You remember the wartime newspapers? It's all crap, you bastards! They never published obituaries while the battles were going on. Only afterwards. But never fifty photographs of dead kids in one edition. Always two by two or ten by ten. Ten by ten, if there really was a whole lot of casualties. Like I said, pictures of the dead after the battles, so that the living didn't go berserk. So that the future heroes didn't shit in their pants. My Kiki and I, we shit in our pants from the start. We didn't give a damn whether there were five or a hundred dead people in the news. Both Kiki and I knew that someone else was going to defend the Homeland. And give their young lives for it and lay them on the altar. Let them shine there for future times. Without us. Whatever the cost. How much did it cost? You know what? I'm not entirely certain that the war is over. It's too soon to say how much Kiki paid not to see the Lika or some other part of the beloved Homeland. I don't really trust you. What if you were to spread it around how much Kiki paid and to whom? How can I be sure that you are a head without a tongue?

Relax

B oris, that's Ela's husband, I told you already, and our friend, he wasn't very resourceful. He got his military draft papers. His neighbor rang the doorbell, Boris saw him through the spyhole, Boris opened the door, the old shit thrust the papers into his hands and said: 'Good night.' When we heard that, Kiki and I—it was one of the wartime Christmas Eves—I was relieved. I'm always glad when my friends are in trouble. You know: they're in shit, you're not, you can help, so you feel good. Except when your friend gets his draft papers. Then there's no way you can help. You just feel good. Because you haven't gotten them. Boris was absolutely convinced that the head of the Defense Office had deliberately screwed him. A guy named Viktor. His wife's called Mirjana. She's a Serb, but she looks quite normal. Blonde. She's got a mane of hair, I saw her on the Corso. Flowing locks. A hundred nuances of color in her lovely hair. At least two hundred marks. Tall. Willowy. Boris had met her one evening when people in costumes were milling along the Corso, and went down on her. How do I know? Ela told me. How did he lick her? What sort of perverts are you? Instead of being sorry for the man who got his induction papers. His wife went nuts, Ela thought that Boris would come back in a body bag. I went nuts myself because I was afraid that my friend Rene, who's a pathologist, would hack him up then, sew him up . . . Instead of worrying about that, you're interested in the details of how Boris went down on Mirjana while people in costumes were milling about on the Corso. What perverts! What shits! What heartless shits! When did it happen exactly, that licking? Before the war, ladies and gentlemen. During the war, the people in costumes stayed at home. It wouldn't have been nice if people in costumes had hung around yelling along the Corso, while normal people were dying and laying down their young lives wherever they had to. At the time I would have said 'from Vardar to Triglav' but I know those weren't real borders, so it wouldn't have meant anything. I know that was before the war. When did the war start? I knew, I knew, shitheads that you are, that you were going to ask me that! I knew it for sure. You tell *me* when the war started! Tell me when the war started. Come on, when did the war start? When did the war start, come on, head without a tongue! Tell me, and I'll tell you when Boris went down on Mirjana. When did the war start? Well? I only know about that last war. It began when the first gun was fired in the little, tiny village of Rudo. Where is the village of Rudo? Don't fuck with me! You know I don't know geography! Do you know where the little village of Rudo is? Like hell you do! Maybe it doesn't exist? Maybe they made up the little village of Rudo. You know what? I don't know when this war ended either. 'Haven't the slightest,' Aki would say. But I do know when that last war ended. The Partisans entered Zagreb on horseback. The horses were white and brown. The girls threw flowers. The Partisans caught them by the waist and lifted them onto their horses. The white ones and the brown ones. I saw the photographs in our history book. When did this war end? When? Come on, tongueless heads! You don't know either. Maybe the horses will still come into Zagreb? Maybe we'll still get to throw flowers into their eyes?!

The Corso. A nice end to the day. Almost dusk. The last vestige of the day is departing. Icy. There are no visitors in the stands. What stands? What day is departing? What's happening on the Corso? Why are you flitting from subject to subject? Calm down. I'm telling you about the icy end of the day, I'm telling you about the day when people in costumes were milling along the Corso. When the masked people passed by, people, presumably workmen, put up pre-fab stands. So that the city fathers and mothers and city visitors from distant lands could sit down to watch the people in costumes. So they could show the masked people their teeth and wave to them, without their legs going numb and their backs giving them hell. Those fathers and mothers and visitors were generally people of a certain age. There were even visitors from Japan. Those masked people weren't just some local garbage. I already told you, it was icy. Open stands. There were kids scampering over the seats. Where had the mothers and fathers and visitors from Japan gone? You're asking too much! Probably to some café or other. God knows. The procession of decorated floats passed slowly by. Every vehicle, large truck, small truck, bus, car, each one was a picture. Picture? What kind of picture? A picture, fuck it. A picture. You've never seen a carnival parade? You've never seen any of the world's great carnivals? The biggest is Rio, then Venice, then this one. The city. These carnivals have a long tradition. And history. For example, one of the things that will surely become part of the history of our carnival is an enormous vehicle (in real life a truck weighing who knows how many tons) disguised as a toilet bowl. It's a shame you didn't see that. People squealed with laughter and delight when they caught sight of that toilet bowl. Including the visitors from distant countries. And the Japanese. And the city fathers and city mothers. Everyone talks about sex but no one has ever said what a huge role shit plays in human life. If it didn't, those people would never have clapped and laughed like that, and that large truck would not have won first prize and entered into history. So, the truck was a toilet bowl, and beside the bowl was an enormous, wide, silver tube . . . Why a silver tube? You ask the stupidest questions. How should I know? Do you want me to lie to you? Would you find a yellow tube more acceptable? Jerk-offs! At orderly intervals a giant would sit down on the toilet (I needn't emphasize the fact that it was enormous if I say he was a giant) and he pulled a fat chain, releasing water, and out of the tube emerged turds the size of human beings. People emerged dressed up as big, round, light-brown turds. The crowd shrieked with enthusiasm. Why? I don't know. You should have been there. Science has not yet answered the question of why a large turd in the icy dusk should provoke mass hysteria. That evening, when Boris went down on that woman, the parade moved slowly. They always move slowly. OK. The procession moved inside the ropes . . .

What ropes? Oh, for God's sake! You've really never seen a carnival! Inside the ropes. There are ropes that divide the procession from normal people. From the audience. From those not in fancy dress. From the serious. I don't mean that these serious people gazed sternly into some distant point, no, only they weren't on the floats, they were on the other side of the rope, they weren't in costumes . . . Can you follow me at all? Oh, good God! There were thousands of people. Thousands! It was all covered live by the City Radio. You know those two reporters . . . What reporters? You don't listen to the City Radio? Only occasionally. So how can I explain? Never mind. Two reporters. Everyone knows them except for you. One has hair, the other doesn't. People adore them. People are crazy about them. Because they spread joy, gaiety and optimism around them. Of course they weren't drunk. Were they sober? What a stupid question! Of course they weren't sober. The people in costumes threw them plastic Coca-Cola bottles full of wine from their floats. The pair of them would take a long swig. But, it's one thing to have the occasional long swig, and quite another to be drunk. You have to know something else as well. At carnival time, the Corso is always noisy as hell. The reporters have to yell at the top of their voices. Don't ask me where the top is . . . Listen!

This is great! Believe me! Or you don't have to! It just occurred to me what yelling at the top of one's voice means. It means to yell from the very bottom of the body, from one's feet, right up to the top. When you yell at the top of your voice, it means that your entire body yells . . . Forget the top! Why are you so anxious? OK. So, they yelled: 'This is a maaaaad-hoouuuuse, a madhoooouuuuse!' And 'This is faaaantaaaastic! Faaaantaaaastic!' Or: 'I'm being approached by a little duck. Heeey, little duuuckieee, do you want to . . . come with me? Ha, ha, ha, ha, dear listeners.' Or: 'I'm lying, I'm lying! It's not a little duck! It's a large drake! So, Mr. Drake, say something for City Radio.' There. The reporter held the microphone up to the enormous drake's enormous beak. The drake was standing on a huge crane, probably decorated as a large, yellow ducks' nest. 'Fuck a duck!' said the large drake into the microphone. 'Why are you at home? Why don't you come to the Corso!' 'Greeeaaat!' yelled the one without hair. 'Did you hear the drake, ha, ha, ha, ha. Ha, ha, ha, if you could only see!' 'There's a ballerina coming towards me,' shouted the one with hair, 'dear little ballerina, do you need my violin, ha, ha, ha, you should be here!' Boris watched the parade crawl past. A spider's web, large prisoners, on stilts, in striped prison uniforms, larger-than-life figures of pre-war

politicians, a brothel, half-naked whores, their customers in boxer shorts, Spanish women, belly-dancers,
a dragon four meters high, Miss City with a frozen ass,
the parade master in a frock-coat . . . Boris felt a hand
on his thigh. Some gay guy? That's what he thought.
Boris is handsome. Tall, slim, with a round ass, belly, I
won't say a washboard stomach, I'll just say a belly like
a board and you can decide what kind of board, black
hair, blue eyes . . . Don't bullshit! What language,
people! Don't be vulgar! You think I'm jerking you
around, that no one looks like that. That everyone is
like you or me, a bit over the hill, a cushion instead of
a board. Boris looks like a dancer from Riverdance.
What's Riverdance? Get a life! You're out of your
mind. How was he dressed? Who cares! In the midst
of all those costumes! I haven't a clue. Yes. He felt a
hand on his thigh and slowly turned his handsome
head. Slowly. Boris doesn't suffer from frayed nerves.
I do. I have bad nerves. And he saw Mirjana's brown
eyes. How could he see that they were brown if it was
dark? Why brown? Blue eyes are nicer! Green ones are
nicer! Grey ones are nicer! Hang on a minute. Slow
down. Don't shout. Boris knew that Mirjana had
brown eyes. This wasn't the first time he had seen her.
They had been at some secondary school or other together. Some GEC. What's a GEC? Get a dictionary.

Mirjana's a Serb. That's not important. It's definitely unimportant. Who gives a damn? Fuck that. I'm simply giving you information. Not a message. Do you know what's happening on the screen? Young engaged couples are leaping in the air with large pins trying to burst balloons hanging in bunches above their heads. Each couple has a number on their back. Whoever bursts the most gets a prize. City TV was always imaginative. Their editors are crazy. Monty Python types. The winners get a dinner for two in an expensive restaurant in Opatija. On the screen is a table. It's right beside the sea. We have sat at that table. The owner of the restaurant owes Kiki three-hundred-and-twenty marks, so he gave us dinner. The waiter brought over a trolley with dead fish to us. I chose a small gilt-head bream. Kiki ordered fried squid. Kiki likes fried squid. He could live on it. It would be his last dinner. These wretches on the screen leap about like monkeys, bursting balloon after balloon. The most successful pair will sit at that table. They don't know what I know. It stinks to high heaven there. In the sea, below that table, all the crap from Opatija is ground and crumbled. It's unbearable. That table is used only by people who aren't paying and Czechs the first time they come to Opatija . . . It's not nice to talk about the Czechs like that? Do you think what I said about the

Czechs is mean? I'm mean? And not the owner who keeps the smelly table for them? Hypocrites! Shitheads! Kiki and I didn't eat. We gulped the food down because of the stench. And left. Have you ever almost died? You know, giving up the ghost, while God's completely out of it? He doesn't want your soul, he doesn't give a damn. He's looking the other way. And you are begging him, take my soul, take my fucking soul, damn you. Here's my soul. That's how I felt when I got home. First I felt cold, then shivers along my spine, up, down, up, down . . . Why should I be brief? I turned on the heat. 'You must have a virus,' said Kiki. Viruses are fashionable nowadays. Everyone goes on about them, 'there's a virus going round.' Only on my friend Rene's marble table . . . Rene cuts up corpses, only there can you establish whether it's a virus or not. Icy shudders. Headache. The ceiling was spinning. The light bored into my brain. All right, I said to Kiki, give me a big bowl, I was thinking of the plastic bowl in which I used to make French salad, for the life of me I don't know the recipe any longer, we buy ready-made French salad now, I was thinking of that bowl. Kiki brought me the large Murano glass bowl we had bought in Venice for a pile of money. I sat down on the toilet seat with that Murano bowl in my hands. OK. I puked into the bowl and shit into the toilet. Kiki helped me to my feet, wiped my ass, married people are very intimate, washed me with warm water, then dried me with a towel and wiped my mouth with a warm towel . . . No, he didn't wipe my mouth and ass with the same towel. For God's sake. And onto the couch. He wiped my lips, I don't know why, you'll have to ask him, with white petroleum jelly. A hundred grams. Canadian. You can buy it at the end of the Corso for seventeen kunas. That cream's good for cracked lips and hemorrhoids. If you have them. If you don't have them, don't wipe your rear with that cream because it leaves a greasy mark on your panties. So I lay on that couch for a week. And read the news. Near our city there's a little town. Serbs lived there. Chimney sweeps, judges, prosecutors, officials, teachers . . . And what did they do to us? Come on, come on, calm down. They lived in an apartment block. Dark night fell and masked workmen entered the building and tap, tap, tap . . . And the Serbs were waiting for them. Behind closed doors. Like Anne Frank. Yes, Anne Frank! And I'm not going to get my head examined! And I'm not an old cow! You get your head examined! Assholes! The workmen broke down the doors, collected the Serbs, took them to a barracks, then into a truck, then into a field, then they killed them, threw them in a heap and set fire to them . . . And what had they done to us? Yes. What had they done to us? Maybe you're right. War is a special kind of mess. Extenuating circumstances. That's right. If it was up to me I'd let all the war criminals and those who feel like that go free. Screwing a little girl in peacetime or war isn't the same thing. Pushing an old granny into a well in peacetime or war. Killing the young. And all that bullshit about young people in war. War is for the young. A ten-year-old kid in wartime isn't a kid. Who can tell what's the youngest the enemy can be? Who? No one. Why should a five-year-old child not be Chetnik shit? Children today are smart. Remember Boško Buha . . . And Mirko and Slavko? Yes. How old were they! And what fighters they were!

Those poor sons of bitches. Those married couples on the screen. They're still leaping about. And bursting balloons. The host is shrieking. In a dress with a slit up to her waist. Her young thigh gleaming. The winners have popped twenty-three balloons. The phone number of City TV flies across the screen. Whoever telephones will get hair gel. The two winners look like two children each of whom had lived with their stepmother. Like Hansel and Gretel, but these two aren't related. I'm not going to phone. Fucking gel. It gives me scabs on my scalp.

Yes. Where was I? Boris looked into Mirjana's

eyes. Or maybe he didn't. Maybe he looked at her tits. Or in the direction of her tits. Who could tell? Since it was dark, and Mirjana was wearing a coat. Mirjana said, 'Hi.' Why 'hi'? What was she supposed to say, 'Praise be to Jesus'? She said 'hi.' Don't fuck around. Boris said hi as well. Get on with it. I get the impression that your nerves are a bit frayed too. 'What are you doing here?' asked Boris. That's idiotic. What was she doing there? She wasn't knitting black woollen gloves. The woman was watching the carnival. But you have to start a conversation somehow. Both you and I know that in a few minutes or an hour he's going to go down on her, which doesn't at all mean that Boris is going to say to the woman, come on, 'I'll give you a quick lick and go home.' That would be totally crude and inappropriate. And somehow Serbian. And Boris is a Croat. A cultured man. And well-educated. He has a degree in ship-building. What year? You're asking a lot now. 'Guess,' said Mirjana, without mocking. So that Boris shouldn't be offended. Men are over-sensitive. If they feel that a woman is ridiculing them, they can't keep it up. And Mirjana didn't want to make Boris's prick droop. No, Boris's prick wasn't hard! You're really in a good mood. Boris isn't a fifteen-year-old oversexed kid. Mirjana calculated that he would get a hard-on, that he ought to, she wanted him to, so she said 'guess' charmingly and not scornfully. Not the way I would have said it. Because I've had it up to here with pricks. And especially since it was icy and drunken people in costume were yelling along the Corso. That is definitely not my cup of tea as the Brits and those with an excellent command of English would say. So. Boris and Mirjana were standing in that throng and an enormous boat was approaching them. A boat? An enormous fishing boat? Of course it wasn't a little boat for hunting whales but a truck looking like a boat. Why did the sailor in the striped sweatshirt throw a net towards Mirjana? Who knows? Why did a woman my age get caught in the net? Who knows?

'Let's go,' said Boris to Mirjana, 'so no one snatches you from me.'

Get it? Male shit. Happily married, he's afraid of someone snatching Mirjana from him. From him? Men really are shits.

'I must wave to Viktor,' said Mirjana and with her head she indicated a passing float. A huge cage. A giraffe's head was poking through the netting roof. Three enormous hens, larger than life-size, were pecking at larger than life-size chicken food. A lion roared. A tiger snarled. An ostrich, probably life-size, there's no need to make an ostrich bigger, they are huge creatures, ideal for carnivals . . . Where was I? The huge ostrich had a little window where his large, fat body joined his long, thin neck. Why would that be pointless? They were costumes! Those animals weren't enlarged copies of animals from the animal encyclopedia, if there is such a thing. They were costumes. And the ostrich had a little window because in the ostrich was Viktor. Viktor was peering out of that little window, trying to find Mirjana somewhere. It was probably hot inside the ostrich. Mirjana waved gaily at the ostrich. With both hands. And shouted. Viktor, Viktor . . . The big slut. Viktor strained for his loving spouse's eyes in vain. In vain. Who knows? If Viktor had caught sight of Mirjana through the little window, if Mirjana had caught his gaze, if . . . Would Boris have gone down on Mirjana? If . . . If only . . . It's stupid to try to guess. It's done. There's no way back.

They went to a hotel right beside the Corso. At that time the hotel was that old hotel. It's been renovated since then. It's no longer what it was when Boris and Mirjana went into it that evening. No. That's not where he went down on her. Going into the hotel was the introduction. Foreplay. A brief thrusting of the tongue into the mouth. A gentle nibble on the left ear. A smile and a glance. Anyway! Why don't you imagine something that you do before putting it in or opening your legs? God, you're boring! A hotel. An old hotel. A hotel before it was renovated. That's where pre-war politicians had rooms for their 'afternoon rest.' You think I'm kidding, but that's the Gospel truth. During their working hours, they'd hop over to their room, screw their whore or secretary or mistress, and then go back to work. At the end of the working day, they'd go home to dinner and after dinner go for a real nap in their marital bed. They're shits? What about the current ones! At that time, in that hotel, there was also a young woman judge who had a room for afternoon rests. On several occasions, she took some criminal out of custody, screwed him in her afternoon rest room and then took him back to jail. Can you imagine something like that nowadays? Nowadays journalists would tear the poor woman into little pieces. Vultures! It's just not possible nowadays. Nowadays judges don't screw in hotel rooms. Nowadays hotels are different. Mirjana and Boris went into the hotel, full of long years of warmth, memories, short, sweet mornings spent in rooms rented for the afternoon. Mirjana blew on her frozen fingers, she probably has poor circulation. Boris took her fingers in his hands, warmed them with his hot breath and gazed into her eyes. You've been in that film hundreds of times. A waitress came. She saw at once that the two people sitting at the little glass table were married, but not to each other. Husbands don't blow on their wives' fingers. They ordered punch or mulled wine, don't try to catch me over details. It was something warm. When Ela told me all this, she said there was something I ought to know. That this information would help me. I would find it easier to understand the whole thing. As though a person needs special training to understand a man who went down on a woman who wasn't his wife. As though something like that could be understood only by a psychologist or a psychiatrist near retirement. As though now, at this very moment, millions of people weren't going down on each other without having been through their wedding night. And as though, at this very moment, millions of people weren't going down on each other, although they had signed an agreement that they would go down on each other at least twice a week. Get it? Ela exaggerates. Never mind. Ela told me everything I needed to know. Boris and Mirjana had been at high school together. Boris was attracted to her, they didn't manage to screw because high school doesn't last long. Unless you repeat a year. In a flash you're into graduating, then university entrance exams, if your parents can't pay off someone . . . Then it's over. But the need to fuck someone you didn't get around to fucking in high school, that need doesn't go away. As Ela says, 'as long as you live.' When you're whacking off, you think of that love from school, when you screw your wife, you think of that high-school love, otherwise you can't get it up, when you screw your mistress . . . I'm talking about normal people, of course. Ela said that Boris said that was called an 'unrealized dream.' We all have one. There have been lots of books written about this, studies, songs, films, documentaries, I'm mad about them, and films based on real-life stories. You've seen that film. It was on television. Based on a true story. A large living room in an old people's home. In the corner of the room there's an old man in a wheelchair. In the other corner there's an old woman in a wheelchair. A nurse comes. She pushes the old woman to lunch. Another nurse comes. She pushes the old man to lunch. The chairs collide. The old woman can't see very well, but she has a well-developed sense of smell. That's called compensation. She sniffs. Sniffs. In the air she can smell washed shirts. In the air, in the living room of that old people's home as the two chairs collide. The smell of washed shirts! That's how John smelled in '35.

'Is that John?' she asks in a trembling voice.

I'll speed things up a bit because the old man is deaf and the old woman had to shout her question:

'Is that John?'

'Is that Dorothy?' the old man cried, half an hour later.

That's how long it took the nurses, yelling, to explain to the old man what the old woman in the neighboring wheelchair was asking. Old people are of no interest to anyone so I'll speed up the story based on a real-life story. A big wedding. Of course John was a widower, and Dorothy a widow. Dorothy's husband, whom she never loved, because she had dreamed of John her whole life, had died some ten years earlier. He had poisoned himself eating fish. They had been unhappily married for sixty years. John's unloved wife had died after fifty years of unhappy marriage. For no particular reason. She had just withered away. The two people, who had not managed to screw in high school or in the Partisan forestry school, got together. Everyone was at the wedding. The old men and women from the home, the doctors and nurses, their children, wills had been signed so that the children were able to rejoice in John and Dorothy's happiness. TV cameras were there and a large cake. And a plastic bride and groom on the seventh layer of the cake. Why on the seventh layer? I was expecting that. I was expecting such a stupid question. Now I wonder whether you actually got the message of the film you saw. What the hell does it matter how many layers the cake had? It doesn't. Maybe it had seven layers because there were so many guests? And everyone had to have a piece of cake! Go to hell! Don't you get it at all? The emphasis is on the story of an 'unrealized dream,' a dream that doesn't happen only to me, Boris, Mirjana. It's a common occurrence. A commonplace. That's how people differ from one another. The vast, normal majority who didn't get to screw their beloved in high school or some other school, and the insignificant minority that either put it in or received it. Take my case. We were celebrating the fifteenth anniversary since graduation. I went. I wanted to meet my Unrealized Dream. My Kiki knew about him. Before we were married, I told Kiki my whole life story. That's why that afternoon, before I set off for the reunion, Kiki fucked me. So that I wouldn't get the hots at the party. The reunion was held at the Pecina restaurant. Kiki knows the entire city.

'That's where that duo plays,' said Kiki. 'The whole night they will be playing "Angie." And you know "Angie!"'

I know nothing about music. I hate all music, apart from Gabi Novak and Tina . . . Not because we're contemporaries! Shits! Malicious shits! That's what you are! They're great singers. I don't like music, but I do know what 'Angie' is.

'Watch out,' said Kiki, 'I'm not going to be happy if that guy humps you. If, while those two jerk-offs are playing "Angie," he grabs you by the ass, remember I'm watching you and saying: "Leave that prick alone, Tonka!"'

All right. We sat at a large table. White tablecloths. The sound of the sea. The Unrealized Dream looks better than he did at school. His ears are smaller, his neck thicker. When we had finished eating, two men got onto the dance floor. Each with a guitar in his hand. Kiki had told me at home that they were 'acoustic.' And 'Angie' wafted out into the warm night. During dinner I had acted the part that my Unrealized Dream was not an unrealized dream but an ordinary friend from school, someone like fat Matko who had been hopeless at history. Mara would make him stand up, and he would always begin, in a deep voice, the voice of a mature man: 'In those days . . .' Then he would make a dramatic pause. Then he would whisper to us in the row behind him, in a child's voice: 'Give me the answer, for fuck's sake,' then again 'in those days . . .' then a pause, then 'for fuck's sake . . .' Get it? I pretended that the Unrealized Dream and fat Matko played the same role in my life. All play-acting comes to an end. All people have their limits. When the master musicians started playing 'Angie,' the Dream took me in his arms. You can't dance to 'Angie' at a distance of five meters or more. You can see that. I immediately felt his big prick getting hard. How did I know it was big? I'll tell you something you don't know about me. On this subject I could write a dissertation, get a doctorate, become a visiting professor, dean, full professor, a columnist in a reputable weekly. The Unrealized danced with his eyes closed. Over his shoulder I saw the dark-blue sea, it was dark-blue, I knew that, although it looked black because it was dark. I felt his large hands, his hands were like shovels, on my small, high, round ass . . . Who's lying! How do you know what kind of ass I've got? He pressed me firmly against the beast whose hard, pliant body I was avoiding, the beast that was becoming impatient and already a little beside itself. Maybe it had even poked its head out of its cage. I closed my eyes for a moment. 'Angie' stopped and then came back. I don't understand music. I'll probably use the wrong word. That music, that night, was a potpourri . . . is that what you call it? I haven't a clue. That music was a potpourri of ten or more 'Angie's which followed one another without a break. If a 'potpourri' is one song after another without a break. Only I don't know whether a potpourri is always the same song one after another without a break. Always the same song? You haven't a clue either. As we danced, the Dream took me out onto the terrace. There, in one another's arms, we looked into the distance. There, in the morning, a large red, or some other colored, ball would appear. If we were looking east, of course. If we weren't, there wouldn't be a ball, but that wasn't important. 'Shall we . . .' said the Dream, pointing to a red Audi. His. And then I heard Kiki's voice in my ear: 'Leave that prick alone, Tonka!' He had said it in a threatening manner. Otherwise, Kiki is peace-loving. His nerves are stronger than mine. But, when people like that get mad, when people like that start talking in the voice in which Kiki had hissed into my ear that evening ('Leave that prick alone, Tonka'), then it isn't a nice feeling. I detached myself from the prick and danced to 'Angie.' With fat Matko.

Yes. Mirjana and Boris were holding each other's hands and entwining their fingers. And looking at each other. The people in costume on the Corso were yelling. Mirjana knew that they were slowly creeping towards the target. Target? The car park half a kilometer from the Corso. If you're not on a decorated float and if you aren't an ostrich, you can reach the car park in a few minutes. Over the new bridge. It's called the Heroes' Bridge. But, if you are in the carnival parade, on a decorated float, or if you are an ostrich, it takes hours to reach the car park. Ela was visiting her sick mother. And a visit to a sick mother can take hours. You have to make tea, read what's written in small letters on the piece of paper. Were the antibiotics really to be taken every two hours, two pills, as your sick mother insists, or was it different? Your mother would tell you that the Partisans executed their men if one of them so much as stole a cherry, while these people today . . . Mother's teeth rub, the bottom ones and the top ones, false teeth aren't what they used to be, Auntie Slava died, which Auntie Slava, the one who used to look after you, Maca died as well, which Maca, the one from the shop . . . The diary has to be looked at. Pictures from Mother's youth. When you're at Mother's you also have to look at pictures from your own childhood. With the dog, with the cat, with your late father's late father, fix the satellite aerial, examine her swollen toes, massage her thin neck, find the Ambien sleeping pills, break the other drugs into two pieces or five . . . It all takes time. Mirjana and Boris had a lot of time, really a lot. But still, people who had waited for years for the realization of their dream are always a little impatient. They don't feel like wasting precious time blowing on frozen fingers and squeezing them. They got up from the table. Why do I have to speed things up? Why must I quickly get onto the sex? I know, I know that you have Atenolol and Ambien at home. I know that you have a mother as well. OK. They got up from the table. Boris led Mirjana to his Yugo . . . Who's fucking around? You've forgotten about Yugos! You don't remember your Yugos? I'm sure you do. At least once a month when you pay the five hundred marks' installment on the tin-can you drive. What the hell! Boris took Mirjana to his Yugo! Yes! It was parked in the monastery garden. How had he managed to find a place in all that chaos? Disbelieving cunts! Because Boris knows the city and because before the war the priests didn't have a motor pool the way they do today. Today every nun has a Jeep, an Audi for going to Trieste and a Smart for running around town. It wasn't like that then. Satisfied? Today you can't park in that garden. There's no room. The gate is opened by remote control. There's an electric cable in the fence. They have an alarm. It's all fucked up now. I have to tell you what happened in that car. I wasn't there. That's always a problem. Talking about something secondhand. Probably Mirjana took off her shoes, pantyhose and panties, and before that her coat and jacket and unbuttoned her shirt and undid her bra. Presumably. Probably. And Boris undid his fly. 'Fly'! Brilliant word! Far better than zipper. Zipper sounds sharp, like a razor. But a razor and a cock . . . They don't go together. Mirjana said to Boris:

'Lick me.'

Boris licked her. How? How? Presumably the usual way. The way people lick each other normally. There was nothing spectacular about that. In the Yugo, by the monastery, minus seven degrees? Mirjana came, probably, and said, allegedly:

'I've dreamed about that for years.'

You see. That's what I was saying. People are devoured by unrealized dreams. Then Boris said to Mirjana: 'Give me a blow-job.' Or 'Suck me.' Or he didn't say anything. You don't have to say anything to married women at the other end of a cock. It's enough to nod your head. Married women are normal women. Mirjana gave him a blow-job. I'll speed up a bit. She pulled up her panties, pantyhose, shoes, did up her bra, shirt, maybe straightened her slip. Boris did up his trousers and wiped his mouth on his sweater sleeve. They got out of the car and stood beside the Yugo to kiss with the taste of sperm and cunt. Mirjana walked to the car park and waited for the ostrich. Boris went home and waited for Ela. And waited and waited and waited. But you never know with sick mothers. Ela stayed the night with her mother.

Why after three weeks or three months did Mirjana telephone Ela? Why had she told her husband everything? Why had she phoned Boris and told him that she had called Ela and told Viktor everything? Why? We'll never have an answer to that question. Ela went crazy. 'I had the feeling,' Ela told me, 'that I was watching a silent movie. Just pictures. With no sound.' That's what she said. I was only listening to her with half an ear. There's only one plain fact. Boris went down on Mirjana. The rest was pain and tears. Why 'silent movie,' why 'just pictures'? Bullshit.

'Tonka,' Ela said to me, 'I'm looking at pictures. In one picture, my Boris is warming Mirjana's fingers with his breath, in another . . .'

Ela was sewing a tablecloth out of lace from the island of Pag. For twelve people. Do you know what a job that is? Hellish. It takes a hundred years. Sewing that lace. So I stopped listening. And started listening again when she began crying, and people began looking at us. We were in the Old Town café, near that little church. A big dog, an enormous Great Dane, maybe a meter seventy-three, was licking the sugar bowls on the tables. It was going from table to table, extending its long, long, long, dark red tongue towards the bowls. It licked them and went on to the next table. 'Look at that!' said Ela and we laughed.

On the screen I'm watching a grey-haired man. He's talking about the last moments of the most famous Croatian writer Mr. Krleža: 'He waved both his arms and his legs, Krleža-style, as though he were defending himself from something. Strange, very strange.' There's nothing strange about it. People don't know things, and they talk nonsense. Did I tell you about the way my gran died? I'll tell you and then you'll understand Krleža better. Why does Krleža irritate you? Jerk-offs! I'm not going to analyze his novels, I'm going to tell you how my gran died. She was from Lika. When she came to Opatija a hundred years ago, they called her 'the Croatian' because she was a foreigner in Opatija. Both my mother and I have great memories of her because she passed away without any great fuss. If you have old people at home, you'll know what I'm talking about. Does your mother wear diapers? Jesus! But, that's human too. Taking soiled diapers off old people. Someone, someone who doesn't have old people at home will think that taking diapers off an old person or a baby is the same thing. But it's chalk and cheese. Shit at the beginning of a life and shit at the end don't smell the same. Old people's diapers make you depressed. You start to ask yourself questions. That's why we have such great memories of our gran. She didn't crap in her bed. At least not while we were looking after her. We put her into a hospital. No, I can't put your mother in a hospital. We got Gran into the hospital through some connections. When I think about it now, I see that my mother was a powerful person at that time. Once it was only the few who could send their old people to a hospital to die. Gran kept crying in the hospital. 'Take me home. Take me home. Take me home.' They gave her an injection. It had to go into a vein, it wouldn't go in, it went in beside it. Next to every prick of the needle, a little violet mound grew. One day, I found Gran in another room. She was lying in a bloody nightdress, the needles she had pulled out of her were scratching the air, she was waving her arms and legs. 'Krleža-style.' As though she were riding a bicycle on her back. 'Grrrrrrr, hrrrrrr . . .' Or something like that. She was ratttling. 'Nuuuurse . . . ,' I shrieked. The nurse came. In films nurses pat the relatives on the back, whisper tender words into their sad ears, while, old or young, they ride bicycles behind closed doors. The nurse said: 'That's normal.' I screamed. But, if you're not in a film, nurses don't give a shit about your screams. This one went away. I grabbed

Gran's legs, then her arms, then her legs . . . OK. I'll make it brief. Gran died. I wouldn't be telling you this if that asshole on the TV screen wasn't talking about Krleža's last moments. And maintaining that it was all strange, very strange and 'Krleža-style.' I can't stand those witnesses of the last moments who don't know that there's nothing strange about riding a bicycle. It's normal. My gran waved, Krleža waved. And you will wave . . . And I shall wave . . . Yes! I'm getting upset for no reason. My nerves are . . . You're right. Wafer thin.

Have you been at the Two Chestnuts? The Two Chestnuts is a bar on the ground floor of this building. On the screen some stupid morons are drinking beer in a bar and showing off their big boobs. The bar on the screen is crap. You know, french fries, burgers . . . Soulless. During the war the Two Chestnuts was a great place. That's where Kiki, Boris, Ela and I used to meet up. We'd had it with guns and ships. The owner was Djuro, not a Serb. His wife was Nela. Croat. And the rottweiler Roti . . . Roti wasn't a Serb. Don't fuck around! Fascists! We always went into the Chestnuts before the news. To see where there was a general alert. 'Županja!' 'General alert in Županja!' None of us knew where Županja was. But we sympathized with the citizens of that town millions of kilometers away from our town. Or 'General alert in Babina Greda.' We all know Babina Greda. But no one knows where Greda is. Or where poor Babina is. We sympathized with its citizens as well. Our heroes used to come into the Two Chestnuts to drink and to tell war stories. How they entered a village. Set fire to it. How the dogs barked. They killed them. How the cows mooed. They milked them. How some of the villagers ran away. They killed them. How a little girl and an old woman were left in the ruins. They killed them. Because one of the heroes needed a door frame. So they loaded the door-frame onto a truck. And what did they do to us?

I have to tell you this. One evening at the Two Chestnuts we were watching *Gone with the Wind*. I could see it a million times and that's about how often I have seen it. That film is great. Really great. I think Rhett and Scarlet are wonderful characters. Figures made of ice in the blue night, jewels in the white snow, a little panda, a little koala. A kitten in a woven basket. Aki when she was little. Kiki when he brought me a sprig of orchid in the hospital after my abortion. Rhett and Scarlet. I could watch them three times a day. That evening, when we were watching *Gone with the Wind*, there was a general alert in the city. In our city. 'General alert in the city,' 'General alert in the city,'

'General . . .' kept running across the screen. You get it. OK. That was really bad. It's one thing if the screen says 'Čazma' or 'Greda' or 'Zagreb.' You can somehow understand that these towns are going to disappear in smoke or great flames. War is war. Everything is possible. Those towns are in the middle of nowhere. They're not your home. But the city! Fuck it! Complete chaos. And on the screen Atlanta in flames, Tara in flames, Rhett is riding through a great blaze, black men scream then fall with a bullet through their black hearts, the sky is burning, the earth is burning, horses are neighing . . . But you can't get involved in their problems. You can't enjoy it. Not while 'General alert in the city' keeps flashing across the screen. That's a real pain in the ass. OK. I'll be brief. Each of us ordered two or three dinners because we thought they were going to be our last. Kiki devoured fried squid and I spaghetti with tomato sauce. We drank a lot. And waited for the end of the film. As though Scarlet's 'Tomorrow is another day' would send 'General alert in the city' to Bjelovar or some other godforsaken place. Why don't you think Bjelovar is godforsaken? OK. We waited for the end. Nothing. Credits. Nothing. Who knows how long we stared at the screen frantic with terror and horror until we realized that we had been watching a video of *Gone with the Wind*, that the 'alert' was ten days old and that fucking Nela, the owner, had screwed us. Bitch. Evil bitch. Hang on a minute, hang on! You think there's no justice in this world? There's no God? Listen to this story about some woman. Look. Imagine an old hotel in Rimini. In Italy. Some thirty dilapidated rooms. And one suite. That's where Lučo and Lina live. And her. Lučo is eighty-one and has Parkinson's. Lina is eighty-one and has Parkinson's and Alzheimer's. Lučo is in love with Lina, he cajoles her, holds her hand, sleeps in her bed. Lučo is terribly rich. In his bank account alone he has two billion lira, but he has never paid her even a hundred lira extra. Listen to this:

06.00 She gets up. Has a coffee and smokes her first cigarette on the terrace. She's not allowed to smoke in the apartment.

07.00 She puts down the iron and prepares the pills for both of them for the whole day. She puts them into little boxes. She cooks runny oat bran and makes jelly. She cleans three rooms and the bathroom.

08.00 Lina has to take a spoonful of crushed pills. Lina doesn't want to open her mouth. She tries to open it with her fingers. Lučo is having breakfast in the kitchen. Lina has pissed all over herself. She puts gloves on.

Undresses her. She's wiry. She waves her hands and feet. She weighs thirty-two kilos, but she's strong. She doesn't like being washed. She goes rigid. She simply turns herself into a rock. She is blue from her blows. And wet from the water. When she has dried her, she dresses her. And takes off the bedclothes. The bedclothes have to be changed twice a day except on the days when Lina takes a laxative. At last Lina is dressed. She sits on the bed. Tied up. She keeps shaking. She pushes thin oat bran into her mouth with a teaspoon. Lina spits. But, something gets into her.

09.00 The nurse arrives. She attaches Lina to her drip. Lina is restless. She ties her arms to the bed. Shoves a little more oat bran into her half-open mouth. She resists. But, she is persistent.

10.00 She puts the soiled bedding into the washing machine. Collects the dry sheets from the previous day and irons them.

10.30 She prepares lunch for Lina. Vegetables, meat, carrots, fish. She blends it all into a thin, thin paste. She lays the kitchen table for Lučo. For lunch, every day there has to be a starter and a main course. Starter: pasta or rice; main: chicken and mashed potatoes. The zucchini must be almost torched. There has to be zucchini for lunch. Every day.

12.30 Lunch. Lučo is in his pyjamas. Shaking. Asking questions. Why is Lina tied up? Had she eaten enough? Drunk enough? He shakes. She leaves him in the kitchen. He eats alone. She goes to Lina. More teaspoons. More half-open lips which keep closing. She tries to squeeze in a little fish, vegetables and carrots through the little slit. Lina is completely wet with piss. She writes down in the diary how many teaspoons Lina has swallowed. How much liquid she has drunk. That's for the visiting doctor.

13.30 She washes Lina from head to toe. The drip is in her vein. Lina resists. She dresses her. Gets her out of bed. She's heavy, leaning on her with all her weight. Like a stone. She carries her to the armchair. Lučo follows with the drip. She ties her to the armchair. She has to watch out for her free hand. So that she doesn't pull the needle out. She changes the bed. She throws the soiled sheets into the washing machine. Washes the dishes, cleans the room, irons sheets . . .

15.30 She carries Lina to the clean, dry bed. Lučo carries the drip. Lina resists. She's heavy as a stone. Water and glucose drip into Lina's vein. Lučo sits beside Lina now. He holds her hand, the free one, and talks softly to her: 'Do you know who I am? I'm Lučo. Lučo, your husband . . .' Lučo had once wanted Lina to be taken to the hospital because the doctor could see that there was something on her womb. In the hospital Lučo demanded that she be examined by the best gynecologist. Fortunately, dear Lina didn't have cancer. Their daughter comes twice a week. When she goes to the hairdresser. Lučo strokes Lina's hair. She irons. Irons.

17.30 A male nurse arrives. He removes the drip. Puts a bandage on her arm, but the hole in her vein remains.

18.00 Supper. Yes. She gives them medication throughout the day. Supper. Lina spits out puréed fruit. She collects the purée from around her little mouth and puts it back through the opening. When she has eaten, she undresses her. She is covered in piss. She removes the bedclothes. Lučo has supper in the kitchen. Filleted fish, vegetables, fruit purée.

Yes. Every second day she gives Lina a laxative. She doesn't know how to say this: She shits on herself several times a day. Or soils herself several times. Or . . . But. You've got the picture. While Lina keeps shitting or soiling or however you want to put it, she spends that day constantly changing the bedding, washing, hanging it out to dry and ironing.

20.30 Lina is in bed, ready for the night. She took one tablet at 20.00. She mustn't fall asleep.

21.00 Lina swallows her last pills. Crushed in a teaspoon. Lučo gets into bed beside Lina. Awake.

22.00 Lučo swallows his last pills. She washes the dishes. Has a cigarette on the terrace. Irons. Hangs the wet bedding up to dry. Smokes on the terrace.

23.00 She takes a shower. Goes to bed. Do you imagine that she falls asleep immediately because she's exhausted? You're mistaken. She couldn't sleep at all without her pills.

24.00 She takes her sleeping pills.

00.30 She sleeps.

She earns eighty-three thousand lira a day. She is entitled to four free hours a week. She doesn't complain. Russian and Polish women are paid half as much. 'She,' who is She? She is Nela. Nela who put on the video of *Gone with the Wind* for us. You're quite right! You see, Nela shouldn't have messed with us.

It's a shame that you'll never see Ela, my best friend. She's twelve years younger than me. She could be forty now, maybe thirty-eight or thirty-nine. You remember us sitting together in that bar beside the little church . . . When that dog licked the sugar? Yes. She wasn't yet thirty then. Ela is a lean, long woman. Maybe a meter eighty. Sixty-two or three kilos. Her hair is light brown. Thick. Down to her shoulders. Straight. She usually wears it in a ponytail. I remember the way she looked when that dog, when we were in the bar beside the little church . . . Her eyes were behind almost-black glasses, her face white, no make-up, she looked at me, and her pink lips, with no lipstick, full, opened and closed, opened . . . And closed. Don't fuck around. And I looked at her white, straight, big teeth. She has high cheekbones. Ela is beautiful. I'm not saying (that would be vile) that I was glad that Boris had gone down on Mirjana on that cold night. Ela is my friend. But, when I looked at Ela, when I looked at that lovely mouth and teeth that are hers, with no caps, and when I remembered my teeth with all their caps, I was glad there were no rules. That beauty was not any kind of certainty or guarantee. You can be as lovely as a kitten in a woven basket or as the eye of a hippopotamus, I think that's one of the most beautiful things in the world, the eye of a hippopotamus. You don't know what I'm talking about? Have you ever looked carefully at a hippopotamus's little eye? Too bad. I only want to say that you can be as lovely as a hippopotamus's eye, but your husband will still stretch his tongue towards another cunt. A good feeling. Good! Then, in that bar, when that dog licked that sugar, and she was telling me about Boris licking Mirjana, Ela tapped me on the shoulder:

'Are you listening?'

'Yes,' I said.

'What would you do in my place? What do you recommend?'

What a word 'recommend'! When I was eating fish in that restaurant in Opatija and shit on myself for days afterwards, the waiter had said:

'I would recommend this, madam . . .'

Crap. I don't like recommending. I said nothing.

'Say something,' said Ela.

'Listen,' I said, 'let's be practical.'

'Let's,' said Ela.

'You're standing on that frozen Corso.'

'Yes,' said Ela.

'In a huge crowd.'

'Yes,' said Ela.

'You're cold. You're looking vaguely at the carnival parade, floats and all that crap . . .'

'Yes,' said Ela.

'Boris is in Dalmatia with his folks. You're cold, but you don't feel like going home to an empty apartment. The radio reporters are yelling: "It's briiilliant, it's absolutely briiilliant!"'

'Yes,' said Ela.

'When you were at school did you have an unrealized love? A great love? A dream?'

'No,' said Ela.

'Were you ever, ever, ever, fuck it, attracted to anyone?'

'Yes,' said Ela.

'Good,' I said, 'great. You're standing there, you're cold in your thick coat, it's crowded. You can't get through to the bus. Boris has taken the car.'

'Yes,' said Ela.

'Suddenly, in that crowd, that guy taps you on the shoulder. You're startled, turn round and see . . . What kind of eyes does this man of yours have?'

'Brown,' said Ela.

'And you look into his brown eyes, and he says, I'm going to speed up a bit now, this is getting on my nerves, and he says come on and takes you by the hand, would you go?'

'Yes,' said Ela.

'There you are,' I said. I felt better.

Ela took off her glasses.

'He leads you to his car, what kind of car does he have?'

'A Yugo.'

'OK, you're in the car, your guy puts on a cassette, you like music, what does he put on?'

'Queen.'

'OK. Queen. I know them. And while the late faggot Freddy and the fat Monserat scream: "Barceloooonaaaaa . . ." he goes down on you. When the deceased bellows "Barceloooonaaaaa . . ." again, you give him a blow-job. Is that so unlikely?'

'No,' said Ela.

'OK,' I said, 'then forgive and forget.'

In that little bar, they serve little heart-shaped cakes with tea. I shoved a cake into my mouth. While it was dissolving and while Ela was lighting a cigarette with steady fingers, and her eyes were two dark brown olives in translucent oil, I said:

'Who is this guy of yours?'

'Kiki,' said Ela.

I agree with you. Although you didn't say anything. It's stupid to bullshit and recommend things. But, you don't know me. You think I lost it when I heard that Ela dreamed of Kiki's tongue in her cunt. I didn't. I was glad. Glad. Because I know that Kiki would never, never so much as tap Ela's shoulder. Kiki would never stretch his tongue towards Ela's cunt. I know that. But, if he ever, ever, some time, once, were to lick anything . . . You get it. If . . . I'll tell you. I'd let it go. If you love someone, then you're glad when something nice happens to them. Life is short, people. If you want to lick someone's cunt, go ahead and lick it. So that you won't kick yourself years later for not having wiped your mouth on your sleeve. No, I'm not Mother Theresa. No, if Kiki was unfaithful to me, I wouldn't cut off his cock with a meat cleaver. Of course not.

There are advertisements on the TV. 'Mommy' is fifteen years old. Maybe not that much. She has gathered round her three 'children.' Why are mothers in Croatian ads fifteen years old? Why don't the fucking pedophiles do something else with their time? 'Mommy' is crumbling chocolate into a mixture that looks like rice pudding that isn't made with milk but some other creamy shit. White. The three birdbrained brats lick their lips. 'Mommy' thrusts that rice (which isn't rice) with a spoon into her kids' stupid mouths. Rice pudding! It's my favorite food. I don't know how you react to aborted fetuses. What you think about them. Some people say that even fetuses are children. Little people who haven't had the chance to grow big arms and long legs. Fetuses have everything, although they're small. They just have traces of everything. They can feel pain. Like you and me. I have forgotten all my aborted fetuses. Although they were children so they ought to be remembered. My grandmother's son Joško died when he was two weeks old. Gran talked about him all her life. Fifty-two years. There you are. We're not all the same. I still think there's a hell of a lot of fuss made about abortions. It's men's fault. Men who don't give a damn about their big children, the ones who already have arms and long legs. And have started school. They need a school-bag or sweatsuit and you have to spend time drawing with them. They don't give a fuck. And they don't pay alimony. They think that the kids' slut of a mother will spend it on nail polish for her toes, and then lift her legs in the air and take the wrong prick between them. They, the dads, can't take anything. They haven't money or time for their own children but as for yours and mine, whose arms and other things haven't grown yet . . .

OK. If I had given them a chance, their arms and legs would have grown. You know everything. Where was I? Those creeps don't even know they have children but they know everything about aborted fetuses. They write learned papers, give lectures, hand out leaflets, show slides, put on films in which you can see little body pieces being torn out in slow motion. The jerk-offs' eyes are full of tears of love for their deceased and future fetuses. They would like to unite the fetuses of the world. Put them on their feet! Dream on! I've forgotten my little babies. Several of them. But, it's a nightmare when you're period's late. An enormous nightmare. First you touch your tits. They are always bigger than they should be. Swollen and tender to the touch. You shove your finger between your legs. Maybe you'll fish out something red. If not red, then at least brown. Or rust-colored. Anything's better than nothing. Oh, sure! I have lots of trouble with candida. What's candida? A fungus. It grows when your immune system fails. And my immune system is fucked up. But at that time, when you put your finger in the hole, there's not even any damn fungus. Nothing! The easiest thing is to buy a pregnancy test! But you know what's the worst thing? I've been through that as well. The worst thing is to think negatively. To think you're pregnant, and you aren't . . . You can't follow me? OK. What I want to say is it's bad until you know. Once you know, the rest is technology. Early in the morning you go to the maternity hospital with a bag in your hand and stand in line at the reception desk. In the bags are nightgowns, slippers, sanitary towels, spare panties, woollen socks because it's cold as ice on the equipment, your feet are frozen . . . After my first one I used to go to the hospital with a large leather bag in my hand. That way it looked as though I was going on a business trip, and I had just called in at the hospital on the way to the airport. The bag was practical because I could pack additional things: liquid soap, a towel, make-up, a bathrobe, *Gone with the Wind* if the bleeding wouldn't stop . . . When you get to the desk you have to shout your name, surname, address, date of birth to the nurse . . . The damn nurses at the desk are all deaf. And neat and clean. They never have a fetus in their belly. They smell good at seven in the morning and they never have a long night behind them, a bad night in which they ask themselves a hundred-hundred-hundred-hundred times what the hell they were thinking of. And just to make things better, he didn't really care whether he came inside you or not. They just don't care about it. One hole or another or a third . . . They come in whatever way you want them. But we think they want to come inside us, we want to be nice to them. That way we'll have a man beside us, we'll never be alone, we'll smile scornfully when we read *Cosmo* at the hairdresser's. Articles entitled 'How to Keep Him.' We kept him! Our man comes inside us, he doesn't put a condom on it! We have him! Unlike the stupid sluts who didn't make their holes available, so now they have to read *Cosmo*. We're happily married, happily linked, happily stuck together, and happy on the machine. The anesthesiologist asks you whether you have any allergies, while the nurse says lower, lower, lower, lower . . . The doctor doesn't say any-thing, you're the ninth today, the doctor doesn't look at you and see you. He was on duty last night, he didn't sleep because new doctors often can't cope; whoever gave him his degree—if his father wasn't so impor-tant, the kid would be a chauffeur in Italy. The doctor tells the nurse all this, and she listens and says nothing because your butt is low enough but your cunt is high. You don't see the anesthesiologist, but you feel him. He's standing behind you. And then, those are the best moments of my life, when they shove the needle in your vein. The feeling that you are falling into what you want to fall into but you haven't got the balls or they fucked you up the way it happened to me, and wake you, and tell you you have to think of your nearest and dearest, that feeling of falling is better than any orgasm. Than a new pair of Prada shoes, than a hippopotamus's eye . . . I could give my life for the moment when the anesthesiologist sticks the needle into my vein . . . But then you wake up. In a room with five or six women. Four of them are already putting their nightgowns and bloody panties into their plastic bag, the fifth is smoking in the corridor. When I come round from the drug, I want rice pudding. That's what mothers are always given after they give birth. That's my favorite food. It's only served in the maternity hospital. You can have a whole lot of money, your husband can be state president or godfather of the Croatian mafia, but you still won't be able to order rice pudding in the most expensive Opatija restaurant. Not at any price. No one could pay that price. The sons-of-bitches don't even know how to cook it. I ate it first after Aki's birth. I can still taste it in my mouth. Once, after an abortion, I ordered rice pudding. I know that after an abortion women have no right either to food or to water or to tea or anything. You can't give a fucking slut who has just killed a human being, who prevented the growth of tiny hands and little feet, who has extinguished shining eyes and laughter and joy, you can't give a slut like that lunch. Unless it was going to be her last lunch. But it wouldn't be. Imagine the expression on the nurse's face when some little slut like me twenty-five years ago asked for rice pudding! Just imagine that expression! It's not being spoiled, crazy or stupid. It's effrontery! Provocation! Screaming! Shrieking, what's your problem, you shits! Fuck you! I'm master of my body! I don't care if I'm yelling this. I didn't get any rice pudding. I wasn't angry. The nurse has a right to her principles. But I swore. Sooner or later, sooner or later, sooner . . . Yes. I'd get rice pudding. I had my last abortion when there was trouble round the Plitvice lakes. Big trouble! That's why I remember! Maybe that was actually the beginning of this war? That didn't change my plan. I climbed onto the machine and woke up in a room. A single. My Kiki paid for that for me. There was a sprig of orchid in a vase. I had wanted a sprig. A soft pink sprig of orchid in a glass vase. Not a jar that used to have pickled cucumbers in it or pitted Morello cherries. I had wanted to see something beautiful when I came round. I knew that I would come round. Few people croak having an abortion. At least that used to be the case. 'Would you like anything, madam?' the nurse asked me. 'Warm tea, fruit juice, anything to eat, a little soup?' 'Rice pudding, a double helping,' I said. I slowly spooned the hot rice into my hungry mouth. But, what do you know about it? What do you know about everything money can do? Kiki paid a thousand marks. For a little rice and hot milk? Why hadn't I pulled a recipe out of the late Mrs. Vučetić's *Golden Book of Cooking*? You're stupid. Dull as a blunt knife.

Of course Ela was beside herself when Boris received his fucking draft papers. You've forgotten . . . You haven't. OK. That's a dreadful feeling. We met at the Two Chestnuts. Ten o'clock in the morning. Maybe eleven. The waiter brought us two double macchiatos. He knew what we drank at ten or eleven in the morning. Ela's eyes were gleaming. I already told you. Two large, brown olives in white, translucent oil. In icy water.

'I can't bear the image of Boris dead on a stone table. His body slashed open and roughly sewn up.'

Ela had seen too many crime movies.

'Don't talk nonsense,' I said, 'soldiers get a bullet in the chest or they're blown apart by a shell in the middle of nowhere. Who's going to drag a stone table into the forest . . . ?'

'I couldn't bear that either,' said Ela and gave me an icy look. Really icy.

'I'm going to go and see him. I'll go into his office and say: "I'm Ela, Boris's wife."' I told you, Viktor, the one in the ostrich, Mirjana's husband, was director of the Defense Office. Ela and Boris were convinced he had received the draft papers because of the icy night licking. What are you talking about? You never licked and still had to go to war? Don't be silly! I'm talking about an impression. If you think something's true, then it's true. For you. You don't give a fuck about anyone else. It was a mess! It is a mess! When you know that you're going to die because your tongue connected with the wrong mucus. A disgusting feeling. The shit wanted to lay Boris's life down on the altar of the Homeland because he had gone down on his wife. Can you see how lousy that is! People, fighters, heroes die in war for ideals, because of ideals, for liberty, peace and democracy, a better future for their children . . . Get it? How awful to die, give your life for Croatia because you licked the wrong cunt! What kind of country is it that has casualties like that? That all ran through our heads, Kiki's, Boris's, mine and Ela's . . . At that table in the Two Chestnuts, Ela said:

'I'll go to his office. I'll screw him if I have to.'

She lit a cigarette. Thank God I don't smoke anymore. In the city they say that only Serbs and longshoremen smoke.

'I don't get it,' I said, 'how do you imagine you'd do it? Go into his office and say to Victor: "Screw me!" If you could get kids out of the army that way, Viktor would be screwing twenty-four hours a day.

We'd all stand in line and give ourselves to Viktor three times a day to save the lives of our husbands. That's not exactly original, Ela. Get a grip.'

'Listen,' said Ela, 'my cunt isn't just any cunt. My Boris went down on his wife, Viktor will go down on me and the debt will be paid.'

I looked at Ela's olives in oil.

'What do you think?' Ela asked me.

'Great,' I said, 'one licking isn't worth discussing. If it can help, it's a small price to pay.'

'It won't be the only case in history,' said Ela.

This made me wary. As soon as someone mentions history, it makes me very, very wary. I don't know history. I don't know anything about history.

'What history?' I asked.

'In history there have been cases of women paying for freedom with their bodies.'

'Oh yes?' I asked full of cosmic ignorance. Too much ignorance.

'Besides, remember Judith,' said Ela, and looked at me. I've already told you about her olives in translucent oil. Judith? Judith? Who is fucking Judith? You don't have to believe me. The only Judith I could think of was my mother-in-law's sister. An old, mean, rich, dried-up shit I don't want to talk about. Judith. Judith? Judith?

'Yes,' I said, 'you're right.'

And I looked into Ela's eyes because I didn't want her to know that I knew nothing about some Judith who sucked someone's cock in order to save her husband from the army.

'If Judith could lay Holofernes, and you know what Holofernes looked like, then I can Viktor.'

Holofernes. Holofernes? Holofernes!!! Maybe you know what Holofernes looked like? Maybe you weren't hanging about in the Opatija parks while Miss Mara talked about the slut Judith and the fucker Holofernes. Maybe you weren't. I was. But I don't have the guts to admit I don't know something. I feel uncomfortable. Everyone around me has a university degree. Kiki and Boris and Miki and Ela, everyone knows all there is to know about Judith and Holofernes, and I feel uncomfortable.

'Admittedly,' said Ela, 'Judith sacrificed herself in order to save her people, a whole people, not one man, she screwed Holofernes and cut off his head to save a whole people, but what the hell, I . . .'

I was in shock.

'Are you thinking of cutting off Viktor's head . . . you're not . . .'

'No,' said Ela, 'I'm thinking of screwing him or letting him go down on me or giving him a blow-job! I don't want to see Boris dead lying on a stone table.'

More ads on the TV. Cell phones. Eskimos are fooling around with cell phones, sending messages to God knows who, while an old Eskimo woman is laughing at a cell phone like a crazy woman when she sees a doll without a head. The development of telephones astounds me. During the last year Kiki and I went to Ilirska Bistrica to shop. Everything was cheap there. Now we go to the Billa market. On Saturdays. You know that little store in Bistrica beside the post office . . . No. You don't know where Bistrica is? OK. There's a little store by the road, and beside the store a post office. I hate grocery stores, small or large. I use them when I have to and if I have to. Kiki is good at shopping. I sometimes go with him to the Billa. So he's not the only man there without a wife. I didn't go into the little store in Bistrica. I did go into the post office. At that time you couldn't phone Serbia from Croatia. You could from Slovenia. For three or four marks a minute. So work it out. All our town Serbs went to Ilirska Bistrica, to the little post office. They waited for hours by the telephone booths. Entire families went into the booths. Mom, dad, kids. Then one of them would turn the dial over and over and over again. When they finally got a connection, they would hand the receiver to one another. 'Is that you Vasooo?

How are things there? Aha . . . Can you hear me? . . . It's Žarko, Žarko speaking . . . Žarko . . . We're fine, here's Danica' . . . 'Danica here, Danicaaa, we're fine, we've got a residence permit . . . yesterday, no, Dad hasn't . . . nor his brother . . . here's Šasa . . .' 'Yes, I'm good, I'll hand you to Dad.' The connection kept breaking. The ones in the booth would yell into the dead receiver, they wouldn't get it, but the ones outside the doors would. The little group that was next in line would just move closer to the glass booth. Not aggressively or impatiently. Slowly. So that the ones inside the booth could see that the ones outside knew that they had lost the connection and that they should be given a chance. The ones in the booth came out somehow satisfied but also downcast. And what had they done to us? I've been in that post office a hundred times. No one ever raised his voice. The Serbs wiped their feet on the doormat, put their umbrellas in the stand, they didn't question their utility bills. The girls at the counter watched them coldly and never closed the post office later than seven in the evening. There might have been a hundred people waiting. They always closed at exactly seven. Who did I call? Was the connection broken? You're shits! What kind of malicious, vile shits are you? I didn't call anybody! That's why I was there! To demonstrate to myself that

I didn't have anyone 'far away over there'! That others had their Vasas and all their relatives over there. That they were Serbs, not me. I kept thinking that fucking Živko Babić had squirted me and that being a Serb was not a state of mind but biology! I knew that! You can't prove Serbianness. If Živko screwed your mother, you take his DNA, they take your DNA, if they match, you can go into the booth and scream, hello, hello . . . Of course you can bullshit all over the place that you are a Croat in your head, who's stopping you, you can talk nonsense about breathing in Croatian, that everything you have is here, that you've never been there, that you don't want to go into the booth, that the booth is already full, that you can't get a connection, yes . . . Bullshit! That's not an argument! That's interpretation. Subjective experience. How does little Jovo imagine a Croat? And what does little Jovo know? Little Jovo knows nothing. Is this glance of mine towards the booth in Ilirska Bistrica a flashback? Am I having a flashback? Why have I started to talk about flashbacks? Who can follow me? These flashbacks. Have you ever thought about that? Do you remember the door frame? I told you how our side killed that girl and the old woman for her door frame. And what had they done to us? Do you think that the genius who loaded the door frame onto his little truck will have flashbacks? Will he go crazy because of the images of the child's expression before the bullet blew her little head to pieces? Will the back of the old woman's shattered, bloody grey head drive him insane? The bullet hit her as she was putting something into the oven. You think that the genius will walk through the door frame in the entrance to his house beside the sea or a little way from the coast, and every time he goes through that door, he'll see, instead of the Virgin, the expression of dead eyes, a mouth out of which a thin thread of saliva is trickling onto a bony chin? The dead child smiling bloodily? The old granny and the little girl will keep coming to the genius in a flashback?

You've got to be kidding. Tell me something else. Who can prove, really prove, any flashback to anyone? Has it ever occurred to you that post-traumatic-stress victims are acting? No. They're acting. Every last one of them! They want more money! They want someone to listen to them! They want an apartment and a job! If flashbacks can't actually be proved, then any moron can claim to have them and have an easier life. And maybe all those flashbacks are merely figments of the thieving psychiatrists? That's how they make their money, get their mistresses, a job for their stupid daughter who qualified in psychiatry through connections of her conniving, lying psychiatrist father. And this war! Who can prove, really prove, that war is a trauma? Wartime post-traumatic-stress disorder? They can suck my Živko's prick. Who can prove that war is a trauma? Why should war be a trauma? Burning villages nearby or far away? General alert in Županja? OK. I get it. It's not easy to tuck a little cock into long pants and set off for the battlefield when it's minus fifty degrees. It isn't easy. It's not easy to fuck the Serbs when it's icy cold or burning hot. It's not easy. It's not easy to transform the Serbs' jerking off in Croatia into the Battle of Kosovo. That's the only history I know. The Serbs were really and truly fucked up there. It's not easy. To wash your cunt, go off to the Defense Office, and screw to save your husband's life. It's not easy. But. Is that trauma? Hold on! I'm getting up! I'm going to look in a dictionary of foreign words. I really am! I'm leafing through it. 'Trauma!' 'Trauma is a Greek word. Injury to the organism caused by external influence, mechanical, chemical, electric, or similar.' You see! It doesn't say 'war' anywhere. Get it? Machines, chemistry, electricity, all those things can fuck you up in peacetime as well. Get it? Then peace is trauma too! So, this peace in which we are living, for which our heroes laid down their lives on the altar of the Homeland, this too can be a trauma. A daughter without a job. Another daughter fucked her professor and got a passing grade. Our only nice experience is going to the Billa supermarket on Saturdays. Paying with a credit card that we will perhaps be able to pay for, or perhaps not. Our friend washes old, shitty asses in Italy. The father, a teacher, is a gardener in Venice. The son is on heroin. The daughters suck cocks in Trieste. Peace? Peace?! Peace!!! That's our peace. We know that peace is not trauma. There's no such thing as 'peacetime post-traumatic-stress disorder.' If there were, it would be cured by war. Get it? I don't know math. That screws me up, and I get lost. I can't get hold of the thread. Not at all. But it somehow seems to me that peace is also trauma. But there's no syndrome. If peace is a trauma like war, but peace has no syndrome—great, I've got the thread—then war has no syndrome either. War and peace are the same, and there's no syndrome. Or better still, both war and peace are the same, and there's nothing else except war and peace. Eureka! Our whole life is a trauma. We don't need post-traumatic disorders to fuck us up! Fuck post-traumatic disorders! To talk about them is like baying at the moon! Like saying that life is hard and strenuous. Like complaining that insomnia's making you go crazy. Who gives a fuck? I'm grateful to you. You have a soul. You understand how hard it is for me to lie here awake waiting for morning when Miki will come. At seven. Are you listening?

More ads on the screen. Fucking ads. Why isn't there a documentary on? Just one. Nothing but ads! Fucking ads! Another 'family.' This time 'daddy' is at home as well. 'Daddy' and 'Mommy' and two little angels are sitting in some hotel. By the window. There's white snow outside. 'Daddy' is twenty years old, 'mommy' fifteen, and the children are younger. They are drinking tea. We buy it at the Billa. Kiki buys it. I don't give a fuck. I'd never even think to buy tea. I rarely go to supermarkets and only to please Kiki. OK. I've already told you. I go to the Billa on Saturdays. You do too. Great. You're joining in. You're with me. Great. I go to the Billa on Saturdays. Fucking Billa. We go in and push a cart. Each his own. What I enjoy most is buying fruit. I don't like fruit. All fruit disgusts me except for Morello cherries in their own juice, stoned, in a glass jar. But I like putting fruit into a thin plastic bag, placing it on the scales, pressing the right key, and sticking the self-adhesive price tag onto the bag. I think that's great. International. I am awe-inspired by any kind of technology. Computers, cell phones, video recorders, remote controls, fax machines, file sharing, text messaging . . . That's why I enjoy knowing how to buy fruit. I know how to press the keys.

And without that, these days you don't survive. You don't exist. It sometimes seems to me, only sometimes, when I'm sticking that price tag onto the thin plastic bag, that, if I were persistent, I could turn on a computer, send an email message, send a text message on a cell phone. Perhaps? Only perhaps. Kiki has wanted a million times, a million times, to buy me a cell phone. For all our anniversaries, my birthdays, New Year's, Valentine's Day, whenever we screwed two days in a row, a million times! Three million times! I refused four million times. I hate cell phones and fiddling with them. I have the feeling that anyone could get hold of me at any time of day or night. And dump their problems on me. Ask my reaction to questions that don't interest me. I'm not interested in those people either. They get on my nerves! Selfish assholes who phone only when they need something. Never just to hear how I am! Do I need anything? Get it? That's why I don't have a cell phone. A cell phone can be switched off. That's why I like you. Because you're smart. If you weren't smart, we wouldn't be spending the night together. I choose my company. I don't let myself be jerked around. Very few people dare jerk me around. An insignificant number. If any! You see, my nerves are frayed. Frayed as can be. Yes. Bravo! You're right! A cell phone can be switched off. Then no one can get me. And then I ask you: If I carry a switched-off cell phone in my handbag, what the fuck do I need a cell phone for?! I can call someone? I call someone?!! You are evidently and definitely not listening to me. You don't give a shit about what I'm saying. I don't want to call anyone! Get it?! No one! There's not a soul on the planet whose fucking number I would type into my cell phone, if I had one! No one!

In the Billa I like the feeling that I am Someone. I go to the girl selling bread. She wears a cheerful cap on her sad head. Red with a white brim. In winter. Something different in summer. I don't know what. The Billa has only just reached the city. It's only been here six months. 'I'd like a warm loaf, please,' I say coldly. 'I don't have any warm loaves,' replies Twiggy. 'Shove it in the microwave,' I say icily. 'I'll come back in seven minutes.' I know that's how long a loaf needs to get hot. Or something like that. I throw Nivea lotion into my cart, a Christmas plant, a small yucca, violets of mixed colors, fat olives with peeled almonds in their hearts. When two out of the six checkouts aren't working, I yell: 'Are we supposed to wait here, at our own expense, for days?! Where is the manager?' I yell. Kiki can't hear me because he's on the other side of the store. He's looking at the wines. At the checkout, the little shit with a cap on her tiny head looks at me terrified. I'm glad that she's squashed into a little box, right in the draught. Whenever anyone comes in, an icy wind swirls round her little back. Lazy cow. Their meat is great. Chopped, already prepared for stew. Ideal for women who cook stew. I don't cook. Kiki cooks. They always have some meat called 'special' as well. Kiki never buys 'special' because it comes in huge quantities. I ask for boxes at the top of my voice. I yell, 'Where are your fucking boxes? Why should we pay for your fucking plastic bags with ads on them? If you want to charge for the fucking bags, remove your logo from them! You charge for bags advertising your store! We pay you to advertise you! Shitheads!' I yell. Enjoying it. The poor little bitches think that they are there, behind those counters, in those boxes, at those checkouts, only temporarily. They think that their firm tits and frozen backs will one day . . . The owner of a mansion on the coast will stroll into the Billa supermarket. That mansion in Medveja. I used to bathe there when I was little. The owner will choose one of the Twiggies, she will smile at him, the young gentleman will take her out of her box, and carry her in his arms, like a fucking officer and a fucking gentleman, off to his palace in Medveja. That mansion belonged to him before the war, ladies and gentlemen! The lord of the mansion and the bitch from the Billa will bathe on the beach that was not his before the war, ladies and gentlemen.

I didn't tell you. My grandmother drove to her wedding in a carriage. I would like it if I could say that my gran was the owner of a mansion like the one in Medveja. But she wasn't. She was a servant, but her employer liked her so he lent her his carriage for her wedding. My gran was a cheerful woman. She laughed often. I'm different. I didn't laugh for years because of my top left tooth, and then later as well. Not everyone is the same. I rarely think about funny things. I don't find anything funny. Gran laughed, when she gnawed the good side of a rotten peach. We always bought rotten peaches. OK. She didn't laugh while she was gnawing the good side of a rotten peach. She couldn't gnaw and laugh at the same time. I only want to say that she was cheerful and loved stuffed peppers. More than anything in the world. Her life wasn't exactly a sale at Rossini's. You've never been to a shoe sale at Rossini's? It's wild. The place is filled with joy. One of my gran's husbands died in Lika and the other in America. Her baby Joško died as a baby. Then there was the war and the Germans set fire to her house. She was left in the ashes without a stitch. She and my mother in a skirt, blouse and heavy boots. For years

Gran believed in God. Until all sorts of shit kept happening to her. One thing after another. And then she broke off relations with him. She wrote him off. She used to say, if He existed He wouldn't just screw me. Not in those words, of course. I'm just interpreting for you. That's why I didn't go to church. You think that Yugoslavia was in pitch black darkness for the church and priests. That believers went to Mass over hill and down dale into distant caves? Young mothers carried their babies to be christened when darkest night had fallen and the secret police had closed their eyes? Little girls went to their First Communion only on Republic Day when everyone else was marching towards big stone monuments. To the rhythm of 'Lenin's March.' Brass band! 'You fell as victims and you gave your all!' And, crash! A big brass cymbal clangs against another big brass cymbal! Listen to what comes next. 'Blood, life, youth, in the name of libertyyyyyy . . .' Crash! The cymbals again! Big! I love 'Lenin's March.' The hit song of my childhood. I'm going to tell you something about your childhood. Listen. First of May. Or Republic Day. Or Army Day. Or the Day of the Uprising. Or Liberation Day. Or Youth Day. A long procession. We small girls hold the ends of violet ribbons in our little hands. On the ribbons is written a greeting to some Division or some

Day. Comrade heroes, or just comrades carry wreaths. The procession marches on and on. With dignity, but not sadly. Because we have peace and liberty and the fallen know that they didn't give their lives for nothing, so there's no need for the living to be sad. They are just carrying on where the victims left off. At exactly that place. How glad the fallen comrades would be if they could rise and see why they fell. You know, see with their own eyes, if they had eyes. If no one had gouged them out before they fell. All sorts of things happened. It was a bloody struggle. Were the fallen comrades to rise, and see why they had fallen, they would fall again for something like that. If it were possible to fall twice. But it isn't. Nor is it possible to get up. Not even once. So the fallen comrades do not rise, but sleep the sleep of heroes and fallen comrades. And then the procession stops. Either in front of the large grey stone in the shape of a fallen soldier with a rifle in his hand, or on the shore of the grey sea. If it is Republic Day. Or on the shore of the deep blue sea, if it is May Day. The wreaths are placed by the monument. We little girls straighten out the violet ribbons. The wreaths will last a long time because they're plastic. If the procession stops at the edge of the grey-blue or Parisian blue sea, the wreaths are thrown into the sea. The violet ribbons float on the surface like dead, violet squid. The living squid are down below. Near the bottom. There were young and old in the processions. Little babies, mommies, daddies, grannies, granddads, fighters, relatives of fighters, and the relatives of fallen comrades. Everyone. The entire village. The whole town. That's why you think, because you've forgotten, that in this country of processions and 'Lenin's March' you couldn't go to church in a little white dress and receive your First Communion. That such children were thrown into the sea to float like white squid! That some brave little girls in long white dresses pushed their way through trees and rocks and branches to a little church over seven seas and seven hills? And then only when there were processions, so that no one would see them? Over seven seas and seven hills a priest would be waiting for the little white girls. He would give them communion in a rush. He would take the little white dresses off their thin bodies . . . No! No! Nooo! Not that! He would put a little blue skirt and a white blouse onto their thin bodies, and a red scarf round their fragile shoulders and a blue cap on their little heads, yes, white socks up to their ankles . . . Because the procession might deviate from its path! From its route towards the big stone or dark-blue or grey sea, and suddenly turn across the seven seas and seven hills towards the little church! To see the priest and the little white girl! Then to throw the priest into the sea to float like a large white squid, and throw the little girl into the sea to float like a small white squid! You're out of your minds! You're crazy if that's what you think! You've forgotten everything! The procession never deviated from its path! Ever! What you're thinking, that's complete rubbish. Where I lived, in Uvala, where we lived, my gran, my mother and I, in that basement where we watched human feet, and dogs and cats going up, down, up, down, up . . . Some feet wouldn't come back because there was a street at the top of the steps so the feet . . . I've already told you that. Those feet would then go along the street in some other direction. In Uvala I was the only person not to go to church! Me. The only one! Everyone went. Old women and old men and young people and little children and babies. Everyone. Except me. That's an awful, awful, awful feeling. Awful. Being different. All your little friends go, while only you, in your short trousers, stay in the square. They come out of church with a white prayer book in their hands and a little gold chain round their necks. Awful, awful, awful feeling. You can't understand. You feel like shit! You hate your mother and your fucking, fucking, rigid gran who acts like a boss to you and your mother, and who fucks you around because she had problems. She lost her baby Joško. And her husbands and her house and everything. *She* did, not *me*! Let her wear the trousers! Fuck her, the old bitch! Why did she take my long white dress and my white shoes and long candle away from me? And the feeling that I was like all the others? Bitch! Fucking! Old! Bitch!

Hang on. Let me get my breath. You see how little it takes? How frayed my nerves are? My nerves are frayed. I'm getting upset over my gran who has been gone for centuries! I'm nuts! And all I wanted to do was explain why I like priests. No one likes priests. Neither believers nor unbelievers. Everyone I know hates priests. They hate them because they talk softly, because they don't have frayed nerves, because they have all the answers, because they have nice cars, because they screw young women who whisper their secrets into their ears, they grab little girls by the tits, they like to take boys' little cocks in their hands, that's why people hate priests . . . Get it? People don't like priests because they're the same as you and me. And you would like priests to be what they're not. You would like priests to be what they say they are. As though you are what you say you are. Or I am? If we were all to speak the truth about ourselves, life would be a real nightmare. I like priests! And I've got nothing against God! Because he didn't fuck me up! My child is alive, the Germans didn't burn my house down, Kiki and I enjoy life. Little things. Once Kiki came across the best dressed guy in town. Kiki sold him three cashmere coats! Black, navy and brown. Lots of things have to come together for you to get money out of that lawyer. He's in the best mood when he's sold a house. He buys a little house for thirty thousand marks and sells it for a hundred and ten. Or someone in prison signs a special warrant to sell a house on the principle 'I'll take what you give.' Get it? The guy has a house but he has no cash. And he's going to spend the next hundred years in jail. So he needs cash for cigarettes, drugs and a young ass. Everything's expensive nowadays. So he gives that lawyer special power of attorney, the lawyer makes two-hundred-thousand marks, and throws fifty of it at the guy in the can. And everyone's happy. His wife, imagine, wears Canali shoes for men, maybe they don't make them for women, all right, she wears a size forty-six. Those are rare, rare moments. When something like that happens, such a little thing that means life. Then Kiki and I go to the Sun restaurant. The one above Opatija. It's crowded. Always. You have to reserve a table. There's a big fireplace by the entrance, and there's a table by the fireplace for the most prominent customers. When a person has money, when he sells three cashmere coats and size forty-eight Canali shoes in one day, he behaves like the most prominent customer and he doesn't give a fuck that it says 'reserved' on the table. I've never told Kiki. I'll tell you. That's a special table, but it isn't the best. Everyone thinks it's the best. But it isn't. Whenever I sit down by the fire, the door hits me in the back. I swelter in the heat. I don't say anything. At my age, women shouldn't mention feeling hot or even warm. The table in the top right corner, looking from the door, is far better. Your back is warmed by a radiator that gives out the right amount of heat. There's a wall behind you, the whole restaurant in front of you. You can see all the plates, but no one can see yours except those closest to you. But. If you sit by the fire, although the infernal fire kills your head, you are sending a message: I am a first-class customer. You think I'm a stupid cow. A stupid cow who wants to be what she's not. Who's burning her back in order to look richer than she is. You're right, of course. Only, that 'richer' is rubbish. Only someone rich can be richer. Kiki and I are just intermittently rich. But what the hell. It's a good feeling! Being what you're not. It's a great feeling! I could spend my whole life like that. I'm happiest being what I'm not. Then I laugh. Kiki orders decent wine, *dingac*, the waiter pours a little into a special glass. Kiki smacks his lips, reflects, says 'that's it,' the waiter pours *dingac* into our glasses, we sip it, although *dingac* makes my ass itch because I've got piles. I know that I shouldn't drink red wine, I know that I'll shit blood for ten days and rub my ass with Canadian cream you can buy at the end of the Corso for seventeen kuna. But still I drink *dingac*. You ask why we don't drink white wine if red is bad for me. Ask Kiki. I don't know anything about wines. But I enjoy them. How can I explain that to you? I can't. You either get it or you don't. Maybe you don't have any money so you can't sit at the table by the fire and be what you're not. Maybe an infernal fire that burns your back gets on your nerves? We're not all the same. You feel comfortable and cozy in your own skin. You don't feel an urge to tear it off? To walk through the world bloody, with no skin? We're not all the same. OK. I smile at Kiki as though there were no infernal fire. Everyone chews his bloody, fat steak. Me too. Fat, bloody cow's flesh disgusts me too. Really disgusts me. My favorite food is spaghetti in tomato sauce. They do it well there. Kiki only likes fried squid. But, you can't come to the Sun and order squid and spaghetti. You know what it's like in restaurants. You are what you eat. Everyone looks into everyone else's plate. Only rich people can order something cheap. They don't have to send messages around the place. They are a message in themselves. If I were rich, I'd order spaghetti. As it is, if I were to order it, the way I am, it would be the order of a woman who hasn't any money, not a woman who likes spaghetti. If you follow me. I hate steak and red wine. But I didn't want to tell you about that. Nor about the fact that, whenever we come home from the Sun, Kiki screws me. Always. Really good. I don't know who told men that they ought to screw for hours. That that's the best way to do it. That it's insulting for the woman if the man comes after only an hour. Bullshit. You can see that in every film. Read it in books. In professional literature. Newspaper articles. Only, before you swallow that crap, look at who writes it. Men. What do men know about what women need? As though men screwed in order to please women! Guys screw for hours because it suits them. Then they wrap it up in 'scientific research.' Maybe I'm the first in the world. What do I care? But I'll tell you. Men! We women don't like to be screwed for hours. You know. On the back. Then on the stomach. Then, 'don't touch it.' Then, 'please, scratch my balls a little.' Then, 'let it go!' Then, 'leave it alone!' Then, 'lick my ear!' Then, 'I'm putting my tongue in your ear!' Then, 'bite my ass!' Then, 'bite my ass a little harder.' Then 'bite my ass really hard.' Then, 'lick my balls.' Then, 'lick my balls a little more.' Then, 'just my balls.' Then, 'wait!' Then, 'stop!' Then, 'leave my prick alone!' Then 'leave it alone longer.' Then, 'a little more, lick it a little more, a little more, a little more, just a little more, just a little, a liiittle bit, a liiitle biiit, a bit, a bit, a bit, just . . . a biiiiiit!' Then, 'why did you do that to me?!!!' Why did I do that to him? If I hadn't, we would have been screwing right now, at this very moment, we'd be screwing. I would be talking to you as I screwed! Fuck it! And why did I do it? What's the point of sex? What's its purpose? Presumably to come and then fall asleep. Or else get dressed and go home. That's why I don't feel like having sex with Kiki anymore. I'm tired of giving him a hand job for hours in the name of my happiness. It's easy to make me happy. No one needs looooooong hours for that! But, men don't give a shit about our happiness! Researchers! Science! I didn't mean to tell you that either! Two priests always come to that restaurant. One old and fat and one young. You're wrong. The young one is fat too. And they screw each other at the table. A dry fuck. With fusilli and prosciutto and gnocchi with truffles. They always sit at the top right-hand table, looking from the door. So they don't feel the infernal fire. As a starter they have boiled ham, the younger one sometimes orders beef soup with a lot of noodles. It's more like porridge than soup. They talk the whole time. Their cells phones ring. Two businessmen. From the waist up. Under the table, their shoes play their game. Lacoste and Alexander. The old one wears the Lacoste. A little crocodile mixes with the Alexander. They rub against each other, stroke, press against each other, caress. The pair of crocodiles thrusts itself between the two Alexanders, then the Alexanders join together and drive the crocodiles apart. Hysterical. I know about good shoes. You can take my word for it. Kiki gets them from Željko, in Zagreb. Željko shoes the entire Synod. The hardest things to get are men's size forty-three. All men wear forty-three. At home I've got size forty-eight Pacciotti shoes. You can get them for a hundred marks. That's half-price. All right, I'd sell them for fifty. But you don't have that size foot. No one has that size foot. Except for the guard at the American embassy. But, you can't go there with a box the size of a child's coffin. Americans have become paranoid. Why did Kiki order them when he can't sell them to anyone? Do you mean that my Kiki has shit for brains? He doesn't. Željko gave them to him in order to cover a small debt. Some ten marks. He would never have returned those ten marks anyway. 'That's fucking nothing,' Kiki said to me. Fucking nothing? It depends on when. When we've got money, then even a hundred marks is fucking nothing, but when we haven't got any . . . I told you I like flowers. You know how much pansies cost? Five kunas. There you are. Sometimes I don't have those five kunas. I pass the flower shop and tell myself, 'stupid cow, when you have money remember the fucking pansies, remember how you feel now, at this moment, in front of this flower shop, without anything, remember.' I never do. When I have money, I don't think about pansies, I go with Kiki to the Sun to heat my back.

People don't like it when those two priests screw each other at that table on the top right, as you look from the door. The manager doesn't like it either. The manager is a believer and feels responsible. It's as though he were playing shoes under the table with the waiter. As though humdrum mass-produced Kiokarlovac and Peko shoes were screwing under the table. As though it weren't his customers who were screwing. If he could, he'd like to throw them out. But he can't. Who can drive customers out of a restaurant these days? No one. All that fuss about the priests is pure crap. Like, priests ought to be more modest, because Croatia's in trouble. They shouldn't wear expensive shoes, put on gold and imported silk. They ought to buy their clothes at charity shops. They shouldn't dye their hair light brown so that it looks as though it's not dyed. What crap! Who needs priests without clothes? What kind of message would that be? If priests are representatives of God on earth, what would God be telling us? That this is going to last another three hundred years? What would it mean if on the altar of Zagreb cathedral, there appeared—don't take my word for it, I don't know whether I've said it right 'on the altar of Zagreb cathedral,' I don't know, because my fucking gran didn't let me go to church, you know that. OK. How would it be if the chief of the Croatian priests at the Christmas Mass in Zagreb cathedral were to appear in a pre-war, mass-produced suit and pre-war Adidas gym shoes? What would that mean? If the chief of the Croats' church looks like crap in a rainstorm, what do we look like? Clothes send a message! A message! If he's in gold, if they are in gold, we won't be in shit for long. Just a little longer. Get it? Be patient! Impatient bastards! That's you! Impatient fuckers! Self-righteous! Intolerant! What would you do if you were in some priest's or cardinal's place? If some hothead came to you for confession, not giving a thought to her sins (which are great and numerous) but her cunt got wet at the sound of your deep voice? You'd keep your cock in your pants? The poor priest has to keep his cock under his vestments? Oh, come on! And why doesn't the slut stay home and look after her kids and make her husband a lunch? You don't ask that? The priest sometimes fucks a village girl. Or city girl. And her parents have to make statements to the newspapers about what they think about it! The public has to say what they think! Half-meter long headlines?! The girl has to tell the magistrate at length what the reverend shoved into her little hole? That's not fair! As if only priests like little girls! As though it never crossed *your* mind to screw your best friend's little girl?! Your hypocrisy makes me sick! Really. If God forgives, and he forgives everyone, why should priests be the only ones who have to keep their cocks under their vestments? Or in their pants? Let them screw, let them jerk off in the parks, let them dye their hair light brown so that it looks as though it isn't dyed, let them get a salary from the state, let them sing, even though they have no voice, let nuns arrange skinny little plaster sheep in long flocks, plaster sheep, let the priests screw the sheep while they're arranging them! Let them! Let them! We only live once! Priests are paid to forgive our sins and forgive us. Who are we to judge them?

Oh yes, I still have to tell you about those induction papers, the ones Boris received. Ela and I were in the bedroom. Ela and Boris's. They have a terrific bed. Old. Boris's granddad the seaman gave it to him. Wicker work. A big armoire, with a mirror on the door. He got that from his granddad as well. And a woven basket. That's where Ela keeps their blankets, duvets, pillows and swimming suits. Granddad brought the basket all the way from China. Ela likes old things. So do I. I don't have anything old. Because my mother was a cunt who didn't want, when she had the chance, to take even the smallest Jewish chandelier. Nor a little crystal table lamp. Stupid cow. Fat cow. The only old thing my mother has is a medal. I think it's 'for services to the people of the third class.' Or fourth. Some pointless class, in any case. Those old medals are all very popular now. They go for an outrageous price in America and all countries where they weren't given out. My mother keeps it in a red box, the original box, in a leather bag in which she keeps all our mementos. Photographs of me as a child, photographs of my gran, photographs of my mother, she was always in heavy boots, and photographs of the late Risi. Risi is a cat. He *was* a cat. But my mother won't let me have the medal. 'Wait till I'm dead,' she says. As though that little bit of tin were a jewel from the crown of Elizabeth I. She won't be persuaded. The woman's crazy, and I'm afraid to open that fifty-year-old leather bag when my mother's not at home. And I can wait. Sooner or later I'll put the order for services-to-the-people-of-the-third-or-fourth-class on my Armani or Aquascutum or Yves Saint Laurent. How I jump from subject to subject! Leaping like a stupid goat over a rocky slope! Looking for grass when there's none anywhere. If goats eat grass. Maybe they eat something else. I like goats. Skinny, firm, wiry, with big udders, somehow self-contained. Wild. Wild goats. If I were to be reborn, and had the choice, I'd be a wild goat. I'd leap from cliff to cliff, from rock to rock, high up, almost to the top of the mountain. Far, far, far, far from people. From you.

OK. We're back in that room. Ela and I. The wicker basket that had arrived who knows when from faraway China was scratching my ass. Ela was sitting on the bed smoking. All smokers disgust me. Especially those who smoke in their bedroom. Addicts! Morons! Whenever I smell cigarettes, if someone, like Ela then, is smoking near me, I feel a terrible desire to grab the cigarette from her mouth and put it into mine. I haven't smoked for years. But, then I tell myself that cured alcoholics tell themselves these things. You won't have one today, you'll smoke it tomorrow. Through the window of Ela's room you can see the windows of the houses on the Hills that are all identical. Pre-fab crap. Some woman on a balcony was collecting washing from a line. All right. That's got nothing to do with anything. Yes. Ela and I were racking our brains trying to think how to dress her for her meeting with Viktor. The one in the ostrich. You can't seduce a man dressed in the suit in which my mother received that medal of that class. Probably third. Ela had spread her clothes out over the wide double bed. Oh my! Oh my! Two silk blouses! Yellow and white. A long, navy blue skirt. A short, white, shaggy top. Three pairs of jeans, denim jacket. A navy jacket, a little lighter than the skirt. So that they didn't make a suit. Two items of clothing in the same color but different tones. If you wear something like that, something that is almost the same color, but isn't, then the contrast is greater than if you had put together yellow and mauve. Yellow and mauve don't go together. But two blues like this? No! Ela is almost two meters tall, or a meter eighty. Nothing I've got fits her. 'Listen,' I said, 'if you wear this long, stupid, navy skirt, you'll look like Lady Di before she ever started screwing. Clothes send a message, Ela! A message!' Ela looked at me. I have already told you about her olives in clear, translucent oil. OK. I'll be brief. She put the white shaggy top on over her small, bare, high, probably firm tits, and jeans on her slim body. If I were a man, I'd have leapt off that basket at once and screwed her. I'm not a man. And I'm not attracted to women. Or I think I'm not attracted to them. Or I've been brought up not to be attracted to them. Or. That woman who works at the porter's lodge at the town hall, the one on the quay, not the old one, the younger one, she has short curly hair. She told Ela: 'Third floor, room six. On the left.' Ela tried to telephone. Have you ever called the Defense Office during a war? Then you know. Not a chance. That's why Ela turned up unannounced. And she was prepared to wait outside room six, on the left, for a year, if necessary. Only, she had to find room six on the left. And that's a big problem for some women. Finding their way in time and space. It's an insoluble problem for the majority of women. Like me. What year is it? What's day is it? What month is it? What side of the world is this? Should you turn right or left to go to the baker's???!!! We're all the same. Ela stopped on the third floor. And raised one hand in the air. And tried to write something in the air. It didn't work. She realized she'd raised her left hand. That wasn't the hand she wrote with. If she couldn't write with that hand in the air, she couldn't write with it at all. That's left, therefore. So she set off in the direction shown her by the hand she doesn't write with. And found room six. I hate fucking around trying to explain the inexplicable. That wasn't the room. It wasn't the right room. That's all there is to it. You and I know that. Now. But

Ela didn't know. Then. There was something else Ela didn't know as well. Outside the Defense Office, during the war, remember, I'm talking about the time the war was on, there were always a hundred women waiting. Hundreds of women. And each of them held in her hand at least six testimonies to prove that her husband was unfit for the army. Such were the times. Ela didn't know that. Women who had not received draft papers didn't hang about the staircase of that building. So that Ela didn't find it strange that in front of room six, on the left, there was no one waiting. She knocked. No one answered. Let's speed things up. She went in. An office. A big desk. Brown wood. Ordinary. A computer. Switched on. A telephone. Panasonic. The receiver beside it. 'And some sort of ficus with white flowers in the corner.' What a fool! Ela doesn't like flowers. A ficus with white flowers?! The cow! She would call pansies, my favorite flowers, irises! Irises are beautiful. I'm not saying they aren't. But irises aren't pansies. If you follow me. If you're not brutes who don't like flowers?! If there are such people at all? If they are people at all! OK. Ela doesn't like flowers. My Aki doesn't like flowers. Maybe she doesn't like them just because I'm crazy about them? Maybe she's jealous? Maybe she'll like flowers when I die? And then pansies, they grow everywhere in the city wherever there is a little soil surrounded by concrete, maybe those city pansies will remind her of her mother . . . Ha! Ha! How soft I am! But, I find it inexplicable somehow that Aki and I don't really get on. And I keep thinking that it's temporary, that maybe, one day . . . And then I get it. Your children don't like you either. Why should my Aki like me! Our children don't like us. You have to live with that. And all that crap about a little bit of soil, pansies, concrete all around, forget that. Where was I? I have a problem. What is a large bone for a dog or a mole for a foxhound, if foxhounds hunt moles at all, if they don't hunt them, then what the hell are they looking for in holes, if not moles? What a moron I am! What a fox is for a foxhound, or just anything for a cocker spaniel—they can eat turds, they're terribly greedy—that's what pansies are for me. But I've already told you that. Yes. Maybe I haven't told you that I like hippopotamuses. I adore hippopotamuses! I'm crazy about them! And their little eyes. Crafty. Black. I'm mad about those little eyes under their heavy lids. I could watch documentary films about hippopotamuses for years. Till I die! OK. Let's go into that office. There was a chair at the desk. So Ela sat down. She wasn't about to stand there for hours. Waiting for someone to come in. She relaxed her clenched fists. You can't offer a man your cunt with clenched fists. That would look fake. A man came into the room . . . Ah, now, if I were going to make everything as taut as a good, big Burberry umbrella, the kind of umbrella whose spokes don't come out of their little caps and through which rain doesn't fall on you like moist dust, I would have to ramble on, at length, blahblahblah, she didn't know, had she known, blahblah . . . Who has time for long stories these days? For *Remembrance of Things Past*? I haven't read that, but I've heard that it's like a piece of chewing gum several hundred kilometers long. Who has time for that? No one! Let's go on. A man came into the room. Miki. My guy! And not Viktor! The one in the ostrich! Fuck it! That's what happens. Not always. That's what sometimes happens. Miki. A meter seventy-five, six, although the guy lies that he's a meter eighty. Like hell. Weight? Kilos? Nowadays everyone hides their weight. I think about ninety. But he'd never admit it. A Lacoste jumper, green, cotton, with two yellow stripes, a yellow shirt underneath, the collar poking out so that you can see it matches the stripes. A Lacoste jumper costs two hundred marks on the Corso, a hundred if you buy it from my Kiki, so there. Brown slacks. Brown shoes. Unknown make. His head covered in dark curls. Brown, cheerful eyes. Full lips. His upper teeth a little crooked, but only a little. Miki said something into the telephone receiver, of no interest to you or me and then looked into Ela's eyes. I won't tell you again that they were two dark brown olives in translucent oil. You know that already. 'I'm Boris's wife,' said Ela. Miki said nothing and waited. 'I'm Boris's wife,' Ela repeated, clenching her fists after all. If Miki were an impatient type, some real jerk-off, like a lot of people in the war, they exist in peacetime as well of course, there are plenty of you impatient types, Miki would have said: 'I haven't much time, madam! Tell me what's bothering you! Who's Boris? Come on!' Or something like that. But Miki isn't a tense type, and Ela is beautiful. Men are never impatient with beautiful women. They always have time for them. That's what I think. I'm not a hundred percent certain. I don't know. Because, however I look at it, I'm no beauty. I never was. So that I can't speak from my own experience. But I presume. If I were a man, and a meter eighty tall, sixty-two kilos piece of ass comes into my office, with that body, that face and those eyes, I wouldn't be impatient. But, if such a beauty kept repeating 'I'm Boris's wife' in a tone suggesting that should mean something to the man, to whom it meant nothing, it could happen that this man would think the woman was insane. War! 'What can I do for you?' asked Miki to cut a long story short. Ela relaxed and said, 'What can I do for *you*?' Get it? What bullshit! What idiocy! What crap! War! That's it! War! Miki laughed. I would have, too, in his place. His brown eyes became two slits, his two upper, small, crooked teeth jiggled. No fillings. 'It's not funny,' said Ela. It wasn't to her. War. Madness. 'People should be able to forgive. People should be more tolerant. People ought to forgive. And forget. How can a person live if he remembers forever? Impossible!' Of course Ela was full of shit, like a well-fed dove or a big, fat seagull. Whenever we get that huge piece of bird crap on the Audi, Kiki thinks it means money. But it doesn't. The damn bird simply relieved itself on the first thing that happened to be under its always-open asshole. Seagulls are vultures. If they happen upon survivors of a ship- wreck on the wide, distant sea, and if the survivors are swimming alone, and if they aren't in a group, they peck out their eyes. That's seagulls for you. They're not money bearers. Vile creatures! And pigeons aren't any better! They annoy me when they sit on their eggs, while their husbands, flying rats, bring them food. When I worked at Jadroplov there were offices with windows. Looking onto a courtyard. And those shits would weave nests on those windowsills and sit there cooing non-stop. I would have taken a ruler to each of those nests . . . At one time every office had long wooden rulers, don't ask me why. I would take one of those rulers. And set off to hunt! The nests and their eggs would fly through the air. I can just imagine it. I can just imagine how those shitty pigeons would feel when I opened the office door. Me. With a ruler in my hand! I'll tell you something. OK. This isn't good for my story. Because it would mean keeping you in a state of high suspense. You know, so it wouldn't be immediately clear whether Ela would liberate Boris from the army or not. But high suspense and plots get on my nerves. So I'll tell you. Boris went to the battlefield. Fuck it. He wasn't the first or the last. Yes. Where was I? In the Jadroplov office with the window looking onto the courtyard. Imagine the picture. Make a picture in your head! Pigeons, or rather one fucking female pigeon in its nest. Warming its stupid eggs. The pigeon coos. 'Coo, coo, coo, coo, coo . . .' Disgusting sound, but the male doesn't mind it. He comes along, bringing his mate some shit to put in her beak. Then off they go together: 'Coo, coo, coo, coo . . .' And then I open the door! Suddenly! Without knocking! I come in! I look towards the window! I've got that big ruler in my hand! Hard! Wooden! Get it? Panic in the nest! Horror! Terror! A sense that there's no salvation! Not for you! If we're thinking about the feelings of the father pigeon! Nor for your wife! Nor for your unborn children! I approach the windowsill! You, the male pigeon, don't want to leave your wife in the lurch! Nor your unborn children! So you wait! My hand raises the heavy ruler. Wooden. Hits you on the head! And you see nothing more! And you never will! The ruler hits your pigeon wife! She'll never see anything again either! How the nest flies! How the eggs fly! Into the dark courtyard! Into the atrium! Get it?

Yes. I told you that Boris went to war. To some little town near the city. Some godforsaken hole. Some Serbs lived there. Citizen Serbs, not soldiers. I knooooooow! I knooooow! What did they ever do to us? This'll drive you nuts! But I have to tell you! If I haven't told you already. I don't give a shit! I don't give a fuck about your cries of indignation in this dark night. Which is nearly morning. 'Indignation?' A good, new word. Indignation? Protest? OK. You choose. Yes. So, those citizen Serbs in that little town, those women, old men, teachers, soccer players, judges, prosecutors, civil servants . . . They were pigeons' eggs in their nests when Boris went to war with a ruler in his hand. Ha! Is this getting to you? Eh? And what do you think they did? You're really losing it! I don't give a fuck! What can you do to me? Nothing! I've got the right to my opinions! Those Serbs, those eggs, there was no 'ausweis' for them, nice word 'ausweis,' a nice German word, they couldn't escape from their nest. Stupid, un-resourceful eggs! So, the eggs were in the nest. Dark night. Along come the workmen with rulers in their hands. Boris among them. Against his will, we know that, you and I and he. Those eggs don't know and there's no hope for those eggs. The eggs wait. Then they fly towards the courtyard. Shrieks. Feathers in the air. Shrieks. Shrieks. October '91. Look, look! I do know some dates! I'm not *that* feminine! Those Serbs, those pigeons and their wives and eggs . . . Some of the females yelled: 'Take me, me, me! Not my eggs!' Get it? What a lot of crap! OK. To be brief. Those pigeons flew into the courtyard. And their mates. And their eggs. All of them. OK. Let's forget the pigeons and the Serbs and the eggs and the nests and the females and the little town near the city and the godforsaken hole. Let's forget that garbage. Why did Boris throw down the ruler, send the army to hell and go off to Monfalcone? He works on the ships there. They scrape off the rust. Engineer? So what? What's your daughter doing in Venice? Why's she selling her cunt when she's got a university degree? Shits! That's what you are! Shits! Yes. I'll tell you why Boris left the army. All right. Ran away. That's closer to the truth. It happened like this. Imagine a room in that little town in that godforsaken hole. One room. There's a stove in the room. Wood in the stove. There's a fire. You'll think it was warm and comfortable. Think what you like. That's up to you. In the corner there's a bed. There's a woman lying on the bed. What kind of woman? Ordinary. Not a Serb, some woman. A cleaning lady. She's lying naked on the bed, ass in the air. Soldiers around her. Armed. Boris is among them. They bring a naked man into the room. A Serb. The Serb has to get up on the bed and put it in her. From behind. The Serb can't get it up. The woman helps him. She sucks it. And it gets hard. Then the woman gets on all fours again. He puts it in her. And then the soldiers shoot him. All of them! Yes! All of them! Including Boris! War is war. The woman drags herself out from under the bloody Serbian mash and runs off naked into the dark, icy October night. 1991. And what had they done to us? You're right, you fuckers!

OK. Let's go. We're back in the office. My dear Miki is drinking coffee, Ela herbal tea. They were brought by the lady who distributes coffee and tea round the offices. There's a café in the building for the employees. You can get a hot lunch there as well. Let's go on, what are the two of them doing?

'Relax, lady,' said Miki.

He must have noticed her clenched fists.

'What's your name?'

'Ela,' said Ela.

'Ela, is that short for Helena?'

Ela's short for Jelena, father Zoran, mother Milica. Uh-uh?! You're surprised? But, Ela wasn't in that office in order to tell the truth and nothing but the truth and land herself in shit. That's why Jelena, daughter of her father Zoran and mother Milica said: 'Ela, short for Helena.' War! That's war for you! I don't feel like telling you about the way they sprinkled sugar into their coffee and tea . . . And stirred it. That's not important for the story. Then the telephone rang, and Miki told someone something about power of attorney. But, who cares! That's all crap. Who gives a damn? Not you, not me. Let's go. Ela took off her denim jacket. And showed her little firm, high tits in that shaggy blouse. Thin. September, the end of September. Presumably. If Boris ran away from the battlefield at the end of October '91, then Ela must have been sitting in that office at the end of September. But, so what if it wasn't? Unimportant. She took off her jacket.

'I'm hot,' she said. Of course there was no need to explain. But I have to tell you what she said. I don't want to lie.

'All right,' said Miki, or 'Go ahead, madam' or 'Make yourself at home, madam' or 'Feel free to tell me how I can help, madam.'

Or else he didn't say anything. Maybe he just smiled. So Ela said . . . blah, blah, blah, blah . . . something about his feelings, and how she understood him, let me remind you that Ela thought Miki was Viktor. I'm telling you this in case your thoughts have wandered off to God-knows-where. That happens to me when someone bores me stiff with endless stories. So, after the blah, blah, blah . . . Ela said:

'I know how a man can feel when another man licks his wife's pussy.'

This wasn't easy for Miki. His eyes narrowed into a thin line. His lips pursed. He probably looked towards the door. The way people look when they are shut in a room with a madman and no help comes.

'I've gotten over it,' Ela went on weaving her fine lace, 'and you can't forget. OK. I understand,' said Ela, 'I've come to offer you a deal. You can fuck me, I can give you a blow-job, here and now . . .'

Miki was shocked. And looked towards the door again. In vain. Help was far away.

'You can go down on me, if you want. Just leave Boris alone! Have mercy!'

It's easy for you and me now to say that Ela was

out of her mind. Now it's peacetime, if this is peace. But it was wartime then. That's why Ela cried. Tears flowed out of her eyes.

'Calm down, madam,' said Miki.

And he looked towards the door. But the police always come with nine cars, their sirens blaring and the ambulance when the hero himself stabs a knife into the murderer's neck. They never arrive in time. Ela sniffed:

'Say something, Viktor! Just say something!'

Alleluia, Miki probably thought. This creature's round the bend! But hey, hey what kind of wife Viktor has! If Miki had the faintest idea who was screwing whom in this whole story. He probably did because Miki's a bright guy. Hey, hey what kind of wife Viktor has! A slut! Who would have thought it! That may be what Miki thought. But perhaps it wasn't. Who am I to get into other people's heads?

'Ela,' said Miki, 'unfortunately, I'm not Viktor.'

Get it? The asshole! He said 'unfortunately.' For Ela it was a matter of life and death, she didn't know then that Boris would go to war after all and run away and save himself, at that time it was a matter of life and death, while Miki was farting around. That's men for you. It's out of their control. OK. We have to pass over Ela's embarrassment. She was overcome with . . . discomfort. Disbelief. Blushing. Redness. The way it goes if you are Judith, you go into a tent, offer your cunt to Holofernes, you screw, you cut off his head and then you realize that the wrong blood is dripping from the severed neck. That's just some guy and not Holofernes! Fuck it! The ugly head in your hand is the head of some poor son-of-a-bitch! Or something like that. But. That's not the point. The point is that Judith went home and Boris went to war. Into that godforsaken hole to hunt pigeons, their mates and little eggs. Which you think weren't that. That they were our enemies. And you still think 'and what did they do to us?' Come on, come on. Don't get upset! This is a democratic country. I have the right to a wrong opinion, as someone, probably Aesop, said. He wrote about animals. So, presumably, also about pigeons.

OK. Kiki and I weren't glad that Boris was in deep shit. We felt very awkward that Kiki wasn't wearing a camouflage uniform over his ass. The only one in the city. Really awkward. We even considered buying Kiki a uniform somewhere for thirty marks, a Kalashnikov rifle for a hundred, so that when we went to Zagreb for goods, we'd feel like decent people. We didn't, though. We were afraid of the military police. Somehow we concluded that it was better to be a living asshole than a little dead black-framed obituary in the paper.

On the TV three girls are leafing through a copy of *Cosmo*. *Cosmo*. It tells my Aki how to keep him. Where his erogenous zones are, which part of his balls she ought to scratch, to keep him here forever. I'll tell you something. Not one of my women friends, not one of my women enemies, not one woman friend of my woman enemy, not one of my female acquaintances—not one single woman I know wants to keep the man in her life. We all want to free ourselves of the men in our lives. We're all sick to death of the men in our lives. Long-term husbands, one-night stands, fiancés, betrothed, lovers, intimate friends, 'friends,' 'close friends.' We are tired of the men in our lives. We'd all like the men in other people's lives. Younger, firmer, softer, warmer, colder, different! Other people's, fuck it!

Is it late? Is it early? Do you know what's on the TV screen now? Now! At this time of night! When lots of people can't sleep. Insomnia is a disease of modern man! At this time of night they ought to show something that would relax and touch a person. A documentary about kittens or hippopotamuses. Showing a hippopotamus lying back in the water even though they can't swim. But they don't think about that. They don't give a damn. If we humans lay in the water without knowing how to swim, we'd die of frustration. We'd need a fucking psychiatrist. We'd ask ourselves hundreds of stupid questions! But not the hippopotamus. He doesn't give a shit. He just lies there, showing one little black eye. They are the only creatures on this earth that impress me one hundred percent. Their spiritual peace is food for my restless soul. OK. Let's forget about the hippopotamuses. On the screen there's a red pussy and a fat prick. Black. It goes in, out, in, out. Why are big pricks in porn films usually black? Why that discrimination? Aren't there any fat white pricks? OK. I'm not saying I've seen many. But they exist. All right. Her hole's full. The prick isn't actually black, but sort of purplish. The color of an aubergine. Who needs that? At this time of night? You're lying alone in your bed, or even worse, with him in your bed, and you watch other people enjoying themselves. Happiness lies behind distant doors. And you want something like that. To pull an aubergine prick into your sleepless body. But, where is the aubergine? The man beside you is breathing loudly with his mouth gaping, he hasn't brushed his teeth so you can smell the stench of squid seasoned with garlic. There's absolutely no point in waking him up. And there's no point in masturbating with squid breathing into your face. That's why I don't like porn while I'm lying here awake. I press a button on the remote. But. I don't like this either! I don't like this either! What's this? The Sudan? Uganda? Afghanistan? Morocco? Senegal? I don't know fucking geography, I've told you a hundred times. So I can't say what this black hell-hole is called. Children's bodies lying in a fucking truck. Antique. A whole heap of little bodies, this is some foreign program. There are flies crawling over the bodies. But there are flies also in the eyes of living children. A large eye looks at me out of a big head hanging on a thin neck. I've seen that a thousand times. While young white women look anxiously on and thrust a little spoon into the black mouth. Across the screen run numbers. You can use a credit card. If we pay up, there will be fewer little bodies and fewer flies in children's eyes. OK. Kiki got induction papers too. We heard from other unfortunate people, we listened with half an ear because we thought this couldn't happen to us, you think that shit can only happen to others, people said, when you open the door, you have to accept the draft papers. People also said 'never open the door!' The papers are always brought by a friend, a brother, the neighbor's kid, a neighbor. Never someone you don't know. Never open the door to people you know? What crap! Who do you open the door to?

Only people you don't know? That's nuts! Everyone kept their doors locked. They began sticking induction papers onto people's mailboxes. And saying that the papers had been delivered. If he didn't see them, or if someone moved them, they would come for you by night. When you least expected it. That's why you had to open your door. That's what I did. Our neighbor Tomo. He lives next door.

'Come in,' I said.

'I've got something for you,' said the shit.

To be brief. I went into the living room. Kiki was lying on the settee, he was watching me and moving his head left, right, left, right, left, right. He was beside himself. He had heard the conversation in the hall. And Kiki knew that he had to accept the draft papers. That was the only thing to do. But still he shook his head left . . . I've already said. You understand that. When you receive draft papers you are not you. You are someone else. You are some other guy, a madman lying on the settee and shaking his head left, right, left . . . The old shits who took the papers around probably got a commission. War! I signed for the papers. And smiled. So that the old fart wouldn't imagine that I'm not pleased we got the papers. So he doesn't go spreading bullshit around about Kiki not wanting to die for Croatia. When everyone wants to.

Apart from everyone I've met. And I also told the old fart, 'Thank you very much.' And I wished that he'd be devoured by cancer or some other disease that very instant. Unfortunately, nowadays all diseases are curable. And anyway toads are resistant to everything. They have an immune system like nothing on earth. I've already told you. He's alive and well and lives next door. Then we paid. I won't tell you who or how much. Who can guarantee that this is peace? Maybe right now, right at this very minute, as the morning is coming into the room, they are writing new draft papers? For Kiki and for you. Kiki has confirmation that he is unfit. For the war which is over. If it's over, if this is peace.

On the screen Big White Hearts are pricking tiny, thin black arms with a needle. Big White Hearts. They help in the Sudan and in Sarajevo and in New York. Everywhere where huge flies flit round dead mouths. Toads! It was great when all the American superstars were on the screen. When they were singing and telephoning. That was organized by the American Red Cross. When the twin towers fell. Contributions were collected to help the families of the victims who were dug out from under the twin towers or for the relatives of those who would never be dug out. They would pour new concrete over them. I really liked that. A big, heavy, black curtain. A million real candles burning. Like the whole of America was overwhelmed by sorrow, in a coma and deep mourning. The sorrowful candles burned and burned. The American stars sang and telephoned, and numbers flew over the screen. You can send cash, you can use a credit card. You can phone Jack Nicholson, ask him how he is or whatever you fucking like. They'll say anything, they'll allow anything, if you pay. Huge sums were collected! Huge sums! Because human stupidity is boundless. Huge sums to help the families of the victims. Huge sums. Then those families got fucked. A beautiful, big, fat, enormous prick, not aubergine colored, white! Perhaps it was the first time in history that the Americans got fucked in the ass the way they are doing it to everyone else in the world. That was one of the happier days in my life. The Big White American Hearts collected money and stuffed it into their pockets. And you, American victims, can go screw yourselves! You'll have to get by, fucking victims! OK.

In the country next door to us, in Bosnia, there used to be Croats. And they needed help. Flies flitted round their mouths, they were made homeless, they slept in tents, thin children got thin needles in their thin little arms . . . There was a gentleman there. A Big White Heart. Who distributed help to the Croats in the country next door to us. The Big White Heart no longer lives in the country next door to us. The Heart bought maybe the most beautiful mansion in Croatia. Or one of the most beautiful. Get it? Flies flit, the eye stares at me, numbers fly. Cash, or credit cards. My ass. That's what I say.

It's almost morning, fuck it. We don't have much time, you and I. Right, so back to Miki and Ela. When did Miki call Ela? Day! Month! Year! I'm not sure. And I don't want to lie to you. I know that they met in some bar. In Gradina, but let's keep this between you and me. In our town the bars are modern. You know what I mean, candles, Guinness, cocktails, shields on the walls, everything green or greenish, old photographs . . . The owner mixes margaritas or Manhattans, there's jazz or blues from the speakers . . . There's a bar on every corner of town. They went to a bar. She ordered a margarita, he a dry martini. Don't ask me what sort of drinks they are. I don't drink. The candles flickered, they sat in a corner. I said, the seats are green, so are the backs to lean on. You know, Ireland but a little further south. If we are south in relation to Ireland. I know that bar. If you go in the morning or early afternoon, it's great. You're alone, you drink tea or decaffeinated macchiato, you get a little chocolate as well, there's a sailor at the next table, with a little peach-colored poodle, the speakers are pounding out songs from the film *O Brother, Where Art Thou*: Clooney and Co. The film's crap, but the music's great! Great! If you go to the bar at ten in the evening, you can hardly get in. It's jam-packed. The B. B. King's blaring. The smoke gets to you. You stand on one leg and soak up the B. B. King. That's why Ela and Miki went in the afternoon. I already said. They were the only people there, just a sailor in the corner and the peach-colored poodle. When was the first time Miki and Ela screwed? The first time? The second time? The third time? I don't know. I just know that they screwed. Ela doesn't say anything. I don't ask her. Miki and I screw too. I don't say anything. Ela doesn't ask. The fact that Ela and Miki screw is their business. Only, she's begun to fuck with me. She started bringing a lot of discs to my home. You know what?! I'll get out of bed!! And I'll recite some of the titles to you! Just some of the titles of the two or three or five hundred titles filling my living room. In the CD racks Kiki and I bought. We bought racks for other people's CDs that are now filling our living room! Get it? No. OK. Listen! I'm holding in my hand five crappy CDs. Listen! I'm reading. Diana Krall, *The Look of Love*, then another piece of shit, *More Best of Leonard Cohen*, then yet more shit, Santana, then another jerk-off, *The Very Best of J. J. Cale*, then real shit, this *Buena Vista Social Club* . . . Get it? Do you see my problem? Have you ever heard of these assholes? There you see! Add another million assholes! Which I have to listen to when Ela comes to see me. Because Ela's like that, you see, while these shits are fiddling with their guitars and singing . . . Hang on! They don't sing! Fucking Cohen for instance! That jerk-off doesn't sing! He whispers. That's how our butcher Mihajlo whispered before his operation for throat cancer. Now he's silent. Thank God. Lying Serbian shit. The whole war, the fucking Serbian Cohen whispered that he was a Croat. Now he can't speak, so he writes little notes saying he's a Croat. These Serb Croats really drive me nuts! OK. While all these various jerk-offs howl or whisper or fiddle with their guitars or bash their drums of every conceivable shape (fuck them all) in my living room, Ela feels that Miki is 'in the air.' While Miki's maybe at home fucking his wife or helping his daughter who's having problems with reading because maybe she's stupid like her mom's mom or maybe she's dyslexic. Miki's really upset about it. But he shouldn't be. One of the American presidents was dyslexic. Which one? I've forgotten.

Oh yes. I didn't tell you. But you guessed. Miki gave his notice, paid ten thousand marks registration with the Legal Chamber (who are these lawyers, ten thousand marks!) and went off to be a lawyer. He thought he'd defend big crooks and rake in the money. Defend big crooks???!!! From whom?! Ela was fired from the City Bank. She didn't want to screw the manager. One year he was named the most successful manager in Croatia. Not some small-time asshole, in other words. So why didn't she screw him and keep her job, you ask. Because she didn't want to be Judith again. We women are fucking Judiths all our life. We fuck to save our husband's ass, to keep our jobs and bring home almost nothing, we fuck to send our kid to nursery school, we fuck to stop our husbands from being depressed, we fuck to keep our lover happy, we fuck to get a dental filling free, we fuck for a long leather coat, and dinner . . . We are all Judiths all the time! And all those Holoferneses keep their heads! The shitheads! Ela didn't want to go on being Judith! Good for her! Great, Ela! OK.

Ela never told me about the way Miki fucks. Nor did I tell her. But she wore me out with stories about how Boris fucks. How does Boris fuck when he comes once every three months from Monfalcone to the city?

'He drags me into the bedroom, or comes up behind me, if I'm cooking. Then he lifts up my skirt and pulls down my pantyhose. To my ankles. Then I can't move. Then he takes me in his arms. Like a fucking bridegroom carrying his bride over the fucking threshold. Then he throws me onto the bed.'

'Just let me wash,' I sometimes say.

'You don't need to wash for me, wash for your lover.'

Boris is witty. 'Then he takes off my pantyhose, my panties, turns me onto my stomach, takes off my top.'

Ela doesn't wear a bra. 'Then he turns me on my back and licks me. From my temples, over my ears, eyes, nose, lips, neck, tits, belly (he leaves out my pussy), to my ankles, then my toes. One by one. He licks all ten of my toes.'

'What do you do while the master craftsman's licking you?' I asked Ela.

'I lie there. Then he moves up between my legs, and licks me slowly, then he sucks me.'

'Do you come?' I asked Ela.

'Always,' said Ela.

'And then you get up and go to the kitchen,' I said.

'What do you mean?' Ela asked me.

'You come, and you leave him stranded in the bed.'

'No,' said Ela.

'So?' I said.

'I give him a blow-job. He stands on the bed, I kneel, or he fucks me, or he comes over my tits, and I wipe myself with my panties or I move up behind him, while he's standing, and lick his balls and rub his prick until he comes over the mirror on the chest of drawers beside the bed.'

'Why are you telling me this?' I asked Ela.

'I don't want you to think that I don't love Boris.'

OK. I hear you! Hang on, you jerk-offs! This isn't a porn story! This is an ordinary, real-life story. Why are you panting? What kind of perverts are you! He's waking up. He wriggles. He's farted. He's just going to wake up. My Kiki. My own little Kiki. He looks at me. Beautiful brown eyes. 'Good morning, my little Kiki.' He's sweet with his hair all messed up like this. What is it?! Whaaat is it?! Why are you shouting?! Kiki isn't in Ljubljana?! No. I lied?! I'm a liar?! Me a liar?! Me?! A liar?! And you?! You've spent your life walking through the world with a Bible on your prick and swearing you will tell the truth and nothing but the truth?! Narrow-minded jerks! What about Miki? What about him? What's with Miki? I invented Miki?! Where is Miki? I didn't invent him! Are you deaf? Can't you hear him ringing the bell?! Ringing! Miki's ringing the bell! Miki's at the door, ringing the bell! Let him ring. There are two theories about how

to behave with men who wait outside the door ringing the bell. The first is the '*Cosmo*-theory.' You have
to get out of bed quickly, rush to the door, open the
door, kneel, open his fly, suck him off immediately
in the doorway, holding his balls in your left hand
the way he likes it best. Then there's another theory.
The 'Magda-theory.' From *Gloria* magazine. Let him
ring! Let him wait! Men have to wait! I think Magda's
great! Magda's word is law! The cleverest woman in
Croatia! Let him ring! Let him wait! Let him wait!
And he'll wait! Because there's a documentary film
on TV!! You know what that means to me! I'm crazy
about documentaries. Maybe it'll be hippopotamuses?!
Animals full of themselves. Sure of themselves. Non-
swimmers that spend their lives in the water. I turn on
the sound.

About the Author

Vedrana Rudan was born and still lives in Opatia, Croatia. She lost her job as a radio journalist in the early nineties for satirizing the then president of Croatia. Currently she writes for *Nacional*, Croatia's biggest and best-selling daily newspaper, and runs a real-estate agency. *Night* has been adapted for the stage as a one-woman monologue and performed in Serbia.

SELECTED DALKEY ARCHIVE PAPERBACKS

FOR A FULL LIST OF PUBLICATIONS, VISIT:
www.dalkeyarchive.com

SELECTED DALKEY ARCHIVE PAPERBACKS

FOR A FULL LIST OF PUBLICATIONS, VISIT:
www.dalkeyarchive.com